From Womb to War

From Womb to War

Lugoe

VANTAGE PRESS
New York

Biblical quotations in this book are from the King James Version.

FIRST EDITION

All rights reserved, including the right of reproduction in whole or in part in any form.

Copyright © 1998 by Lugoe

Published by Vantage Press, Inc.
516 West 34th Street, New York, New York 10001

Manufactured in the United States of America
ISBN: 0-533-12674- 6

Library of Congress Catalog Card No.: 97-91439

0 9 8 7 6 5 4 3 2 1

Contents

1. God, Church, Clothing, Prohibition, Cats 1
2. Deliverymen, Horses, Inelegant Expressions 24
3. Games, City Market 45
4. Early Sex, Personality, Fermat's Theorem 62
5. Automobiles, Streetcars, Entertainments, Puzzles 73
6. Physicians, Buttocks, and Genitalia in Language 92
7. The Times, "Ass" in Speech, Workaday World 98
8. Fear of the Dark 110
9. Homosexuality, Lightning, Ditties, Jokes, Tomato Paste, Home Brew, Anisette 119
10. Puppy Love, The Great Depression, Puberty 129
11. My Father, Church and Police, in the Hospital 139
12. The Times, Bordello Visits, CCC, First Job 145
13. In the Army, Invisible Blacks, Recruit Life 161
14. By Ship from New York to San Francisco 175
15. Fort McDowell and San Francisco 188
16. To Hawaii, Luke Field, Squadron Life 197
17. Loss of Virginity, Manual for the Courts-Martial 211
18. Dog Tags, God, Gas Masks 217
19. In California, Japanese Attack Hawaii, March Field, Debtor God 225

From Womb to War

1
God, Church, Clothing, Prohibition, Cats

I first met God in a whorehouse in Honolulu. He was suspended by His armpits between two giant military policemen (MPs) who were carrying Him down the stairs from the second-floor action room of the brothel. I was heading up the stairs.

He hung limply on His "crutches," all four limbs swaying as though boneless, and His drooping head rolled from side to side with each downward step by His bearers. He was small, with a thin face, very dark complexion, dark brown eyes, and curly jet black hair—and He was drunk; slack-jawed, glassyeyed drunk.

He is swaying like a standard carried in a parade, I thought at first glance, but then I was overcome by a very different, and vivid, impression. "No," I said as I drew in a quick breath and my heart raced. "He . . . looks exactly like a crucified Christ—like so many of those depictions." Of course, He's not suspended from a cross or a stake or a tree (take your choice, if you read the Bible), but from a pair of parallel bars, in effect.

I stepped to one side to let the trio pass, and as I did so God caught my eye. "I love you, Lugoe!" He said, slurring his ls.

"Don't pay any attention to this queer," snarled one of the MPs. "He says that to everybody."

But I remained frozen in amazement. How did He know my name? After some hard thought trying to remember whether I had ever met Him somewhere, I shrugged it off and proceeded up the stairs. It was my night for "around the world."

(Perhaps, before going any further, I should fill you in on how I came to be there—not in the cathouse or Honolulu but in the Hawaiian Islands. Well, if you are comfortable, and in the mood to listen, it was like this. [I'll try not to get into too much detail.]).

I was born in a coal-mining town—soft coal—in western Pennsylvania in 1918. (Stop groaning; I told you I won't go into very much detail.) My parents were emigrants from southern Italy (Apulia) who arrived shortly after the turn of the century. As I got the story, in due time, my father's wealthy parents had forbidden his marriage to my mother, whose family was poor. My father defied his parents' wishes, marrying my mother, was disowned by his family, and sailed with his wife to the land reputed to be a first cousin to Shangri-la.

Whoever recruited my father for toil in the New World had intended him for labor in the vineyards of California. However, my father met friends in New York City who induced him to join their group destined for the coal mines of Pennsylvania. A year after my birth, recruiters for the newly electrified industrial plants of western New York raided the mines for workers and, figuratively, captured my father among others. So that brings me to the start of my story, and I'll begin with one of my earliest memories, at about age four. (. . . Shut up! And listen.)

My mother drew me over to the kitchen window so that, with her blue eyes, she could get a good look into my blue eyes. Then, very calmly and enunciating carefully, she proceeded to tell me about God. After about a minute and a half of listening to discourse on a vague Creature hovering up there in the sky and keeping track of everything going on down here and having subjected each misstatement to logical evaluation, I calmly said to myself as I continued to look my mother straight in the eye without changing my expression, "Bullshit." Five minutes and two more "bullshits" later, my mother ended her soft lecture. We had been locked eye to eye the full time, and at the end there was a moment of silence as she waited for my response. I gave none, and she turned away as expressionless as I, seemingly unconcerned as to whether or not the seeds she had sown had fallen on fertile soil. And she never spoke to me of religion again.

I puzzled over why my mother had felt compelled to give me the God lecture, because I felt that she was, as I, a rational person. Did she feel it was the duty expected of a mother and necessary to conform? Or did she do it out of a sense of loyalty to her husband—my father—who was a religious fanatic?

And speaking of my father's religious fanaticism (he forced his family to church seven days a week, twice on Sundays), it was born of, or transferred with, his conversion from Roman Catholicism to Protestantism. He had a high contempt for his former religion and often spoke bitterly of its adherents, saying, "No telling how many dog bones they have kissed, believing them to be bones of saints." To my great regret now, I never asked my father how and when he had come to the realization that he had been duped by the Roman Catholic Church. And I ached to ask whether he might not be being duped again, by another religion. But I didn't dare. He was too emotional about his religion.

In fact, his new religion so exhilarated him that one day he decided to throw a religious tantrum. It must have been a Saturday because he was neither at work nor at church and he was shirtless and barefoot. It began in the morning and ended up in the afternoon with him in jail. It started with his raising his head and his voice upward and talking to God. Apparently, God was giving him instructions, telling my father to position his family members in various locations in the house and specifying whether they be sitting or standing, and also ordering my father to break windows at various intervals, which my father did with relish, using the handle of a broom for that purpose.

He would take a family member, me for example, and placing a chair at random in, say, the middle room would order, "Sit here." Then he would cock his head skyward in a listening attitude for a moment and, apparently on instruction, have me move the chair three feet to one side. Another listen, and he would have me stand beside the chair. Having it right finally, he would position another family member (there were four of the children in the house at the time) in the kitchen or in the front room. In between positionings, which were changed frequently, he would thoroughly demolish a windowpane, upper or lower, with several strokes of the broomstick.

But not so for the upper pane of the kitchen window. I was behind him in the kitchen at the time when he picked up an unopened tin of canned food, balancing it and taking the measure of this target as carefully as David, before Goliath, did with the rock in his sling. Then my father hurled the can endwise through the kitchen window's upper pane. To my astonishment, a perfectly round hole, the diameter of the can, appeared in the windowpane. A few fine cracks radiated on the otherwise-intact glass. What a marvelous feat!

But, I thought, by now there must be outside the house a crowd of people attracted by the recurring sounds of this smashing glass. So when I got the opportunity, while my father was positioning someone in the kitchen and I was in the middle room, I dropped to all fours and crawled to one of the broken front room windows and peeked over the windowsill. Yes, there was a crowd out there, about twenty or thirty people on the sidewalks and in the street, all staring wide-eyed at the house.

I beat a hasty retreat to the middle room, where my mother was sitting on a couch and my father was standing in front of her. He had his head raised to the sky (I don't think the intervening ceiling and roof of the house interfered with his vision), and *he* was giving instructions to *God*. "Tell her [meaning my mother] to speak," he ordered God. My father waited a few seconds; my mother remained silent, and he repeated imperiously, "Tell her to speak!"

In fear and desperation my mother spoke. "Praise the Lord!" she said. I should mention that this expression was standard for filling lulls in conversations and for helping along boring periods in church. When the preacher or a member making a long testimony paused for a breath, one or more of the congregation would shout, "Praise the Lord!" and this ejaculation would be followed by scattered outbursts of, "Amen!" Also, the practice helped these poor people who performed hard physical work and for long hours (the eight-hour day was yet to come) to stay awake, especially on hot summer evenings. Air-conditioning was a long way in the future.

This ordeal by faith, trying to stay awake in church for two hours every evening of the week from seven to nine o'clock, was simply too much for one church member who had the wonderful capacity to fall asleep instantly whenever he wished and in any position. He attended church regularly and each night slept through the two hours religiously, sitting straight up and with chin high in an attitude of attention but with his eyes closed. The long, hard wooden benches didn't bother him a bit. He did this for years except for one night when, sitting next to the aisle, he had the indiscretion to snore a little bit. One of the elders, who was sitting two rows of benches up toward the front of the church and next to the opposite side of the aisle, lost control of himself when, during a sudden silence, the church member had the floor, so to speak. The furious elder turned and hurled his softbound Bible diagonally across the aisle, bouncing it off the church member's knee. That act caused him to waken, and he remained so for a good ten minutes. It marred a longtime record of devotional sleep.

(Let's see; where was I? Oh, yeah!) This expression, "Praise the Lord!," was also used as a greeting when church members met, in private or in public. A church member, encountering my father and mother on the street, would say to my father, "Praise the Lord, Brother," and with a lift of the hat and a little bow to my mother, "Praise the Lord, Sister." And my parents would respond, "Amen, Brother."

So, you see why, when bidden to speak by God—at my addled father's order—my mother uttered the handy-for-all-occasions, "Praise the Lord!" Actually, she said, "Gloria a Gesù [glory to Jesus]!," as did all the church members when speaking in Italian; the bilingual members when speaking English always used, "Praise the Lord!" (In later years the church services, which were all conducted in Italian—except for Sunday school—alternated daily between Italian and English and eventually became English-only.)

(Just let me finish about the church and then I'll go back to my father's tantrum. And when I do, you'll see why I call it a tantrum. Here, have a beer; maybe you'll stop sighing.)

The hardest part about church, and this is a deliberate pun, was the plain wooden floor upon which we knelt for prayer, while we rested our forearms on the plain wooden benches where we had been sitting. These prayer sessions lasted about a half hour and might go on longer, depending on the will of the prayer(s). The praying was done aloud by anyone who wished and in sequence by everyone who wished and for as long as they wished. There were two limiting factors (barring a fire, other emergencies, or acts of God, of course): the excruciating pain of knees against the hardwood floor; and the rambling or long-winded or extremely boring or unacceptable or even frightening prayers, which the minister judiciously curtailed.

After about ten minutes of kneeling, the women knelt on their purses (those with babies spent the time in the women's rest room area), the men knelt on their Bibles, and the children did the best they could with handkerchiefs under their knees. I should mention that "speaking in tongues" (glossolalia) was considered prayer and was encouraged, perhaps for its entertainment value. This ecstatic or apparently ecstatic utterance of unintelligible speechlike sounds was said to be caused by the descent of the Holy Spirit upon one, and it usually began with a low murmur as the performer—I'm sorry, the utterer—accepted the Holy Spirit into his body. (Was the pain of cracking kneecaps a catalyst for all this?)

As soon as the congregation caught the low murmur,

it poured out encouragement: "Hallelujah! Praise the Lord! Bless you!" at which the murmurer would vocalize more loudly and more quickly into a babbling; the congregation would increase its volume of encouragement (it was as though they were urging, "Go, go, go, go!"), and the babbler would then go into a still-louder and more rapid vocalization of gibberish. All speakers in tongues differed in style and language and were listened to with great interest, if not fascination. One woman was different enough to merit anticipation of her "speeches." Her voice would rise to a high pitch, and she would repeat at odd intervals: "TSEEPEE TSEEPEE LOPPIE LOPPIE." This language struck the congregation as hilarious, and there would be titters and the choking sounds of strangled laughter. It struck me as sad.

One last word about my father's church: the Sunday school. The children would be assigned to teachers, six to ten pupils for each teacher, and the teacher-pupil groups were scattered throughout the big open room of the church. As I have intimated, I, like all children, was born an atheist, "without a God." These teachers intended to provide me with one, and for this purpose they read from a book called the Holy Bible, a fantasia of history, biography, pornography, grisly folk tales, esoterica, and supernatural beings, one of which was a demented God, one of the most repulsive and despicable characters I have ever encountered in fiction or nonfiction. And I (and the other captive children in my group) was admonished to put my unquestioning faith and trust in this Monster, to abandon reason and to believe in Him blindly, to crawl to Him, to utter loud praise to Him, to tell Him I was no good, not worthy, to live in fear of Him, and to love Him!

And I would stare in wide-eyed amazement as I listened incredulously to absurd stories from the Bible, because the teacher was presenting them as true. There was no twinkle in the eye to indicate, "Isn't this an entertaining story?" There was no little smile to say, "Talk about tall tales!" It was deadly serious business. I felt so sorry for the teacher, so sad that a grown-up could treat such things seriously.

In summary, the church service would go like this. (What? Yes, I said the Sunday school would be the last thing. It was. I'm just summarizing, OK?) The preacher would call for a song, and a member would suggest the number of a song in the songbook. In case two (or more) members spoke up simultaneously, the preacher asked for a consensus on which song to sing. All sang in unison. After the song the preacher read some selected verses from the Bible and made a brief commentary. Next came testimonials by anyone who wished. These were delivered standing in place and usually revealed how the testifier had come "to see the light." Then came a song, followed by the main event of the evening: the sermon. Then two or three songs, often warlike ("Onward Christian Soldiers" and "Raise, Raise the Banner!"), followed by prayer as I described, and finally a song with everyone standing. Many English hymns were translated into Italian and incorporated into the Italian songbook, and many of the Italian songs were translated into English for the songbooks used on the nights when the service was in English. I remember the song beginning, "Let us gather by the river," which I would paraphrase to myself, to relieve my boredom, "Let us get her by the river, let us grab her by the ass, . . . " et cetera.

And now, back to my father and his religious tantrum. When, at my father's command, God caused my mother to speak and she said, "Praise the Lord!" my father slapped her, but very lightly. Actually, he brushed her cheek with his fingertips as he said, "Be still." Then he looked upward and ordered God again to make her speak, and when she spoke he "slapped" her again and ordered her to be still.

"Aha!" I said to myself, noting his tender slap. "He has himself under control; my father is having himself a Roman holiday by terrorizing his family." The whole episode was repeated once more. And now we come to the denouement. My father lined up everyone in the house in single file, starting with me in the kitchen, my mother and older sister in the middle room, and two brothers in the front room. As my father was positioning the last family member at the front of the house, I looked down the line of living statues and noted that we formed a perfectly straight line. But while my father's back was toward us, my sister jumped out of line and dashed through the middle room, through the kitchen, down the kitchen stairs, around the house, and to the nearby grocery store, from which she telephoned the police.

In no time at all a patrol wagon arrived out front and three huge Irish cops entered the house with my sister. My father sat himself calmly on the front room couch and softly, sadly, spoke my sister's name twice to chide her for her act. The cop who seemed to be in charge stood in front of my father and looked down at him silently, then said to my father, "Why don't you have your shirt on?" I translated that into Italian.

My father thought it over for a moment; then he answered calmly, "Because I don't feel cold."

Nice, I thought.

The cop thought so, too, I believe. After a few moments of steady gazing at my perfectly-at-ease father, the cop came up with question number two: "Why don't you have your socks and shoes on?"

With no hesitation this time, my father said, "I feel comfortable this way."

Very good! I thought. Apparently, the questioner thought so, too. He seemed unsure as he closely eyed the seemingly perfectly normal and relaxed person seated before him. But then there were the broken windows and the shards of glass on the floors of all the rooms.

He made up his mind. "Take him!" he said to the two giants standing by, and instantly they each put a hand under my father's arms, lifted him off the couch, and walked him in his bare feet through the broken glass, out of the house, and into the paddy wagon.

When I came home from Sunday school the next morning there was my father sitting all dressed up, including tie and jacket, in a straight-backed chair, in front of the warm kitchen stove. He was fast asleep and seemed to be enjoying it. My mother smiled at me happily to indicate that everything was all right. And it was; my father never threw another tantrum. Three big Irish cops and a night in jail were more than enough for God and man.

(Well, that's about it for my early religious experience. Of course I left a lot out. . . . And you appreciate it? I'll try to do the same for my secular encounters with the world.)

Really, my very earliest memory is of the family's moving into the house that would become our permanent residence. And the memory begins with my helping to carry small articles into the house from the vehicle at the curb while curious neighbors stood by to watch. I remember my embarrassment at the snickers of the neighborhood children as it fell to my lot to carry in a chamber pot. In many houses, toilets were in the cellar (I'm talking about the year 1921 or 1922, and to avoid making a long trip during the night or very early morning, chamber pots were kept beside or under the bed.)

There was a potbellied stove for heating the house, a two-burner kerosene stove for cooking, and a kerosene lamp for the middle room to supplement the dim incandescent lamps in the other rooms of the house. These were replaced before long with a coal-burning furnace for central heating, a coal- or wood-burning range for cooking, and brighter incandescent lamps for lighting.

My next vivid memory concerns shoes, which were expensive items. A few weeks after we moved in, my father purchased two secondhand pairs of high-button shoes for me and my older brother. These were really beautiful shoes. They extended to just above the ankle, and mine were gray suede, each shoe with a row of red buttons (they were spheres) attached to one quarter of a shoe by one-inch-long cords, and they were pulled by means of a handled hook through the corresponding eyelets on the other quarter. The hooks were often works of art, almost jewelry, with plated hooks and plain or fancy handles of various materials. Unfortunately for my father, such shoes were out of style. After one day of ridicule from our "gangs" (our circles of neighborhood children) my brother and I absolutely refused to wear the shoes. My father was forced to buy the conventional Oxford shoes—and a last, hammer, awl, nails, knives (and sharpening stones), leather, and leather stain to keep the shoes in repair.

Since I'm on the subject of wear, let me note briefly what I saw being worn at the time. Knickers were still in style, but in steadily fewer numbers and, finally, worn only by some golfers. These loose trousers terminated in tight cuffs that, when pulled up to just below the knees, supported the overhang of the trouser legs, the overhang extending down to about midcalf. They looked sporty.

To be honest about it, I never saw any woman—or girl—in full-fledged flapper attire. The word *flapper* may have originated from the habit of unconventional girls of leaving their galoshes unbuckled in wintertime, which condition resulted in a flapping sound as the girls walked. Occasionally there would appear a cloche hat on some woman in her thirties, say, or a knee-high skirt on someone in her early twenties. Bold girls rolled their stockings down to just below the knee so that the roll was visible. One less bold wore the roll just above the knee and lifted her skirt to show you that she was a little naughty. Generally, dresses were shaped and hung to just below the knee for girls and young women, to almost midcalf for women in the late twenties to late thirties, to about eight inches from the ground for older women and four inches from the ground for elderly women.

These last, if they were Italian, were wont to say of the young generation, "Se mostra la gamba, mostra il culo," which translates to, "If she shows her leg, she'll show her ass." Among these last, also, were my kindergarten teachers, who fulfilled the essential qualification for the job, that of being a venerable grandmother. With each higher grade in school, the teachers were younger and prettier and their skirts were shorter, until, in high school, it was difficult to distinguish a teacher from a pupil except from the loud whistling in hallways by the boys at the teachers. You should consider that the passing years had to do with these progressive changes. Incidentally, teachers in my grade school years were all females except for the music teacher who visited the class for one hour each week and the shop teacher, who taught woodwork. In junior high school, all shop teachers were men, so were the boys' gymnasium and swimming teachers, and so was one mathematics teacher. In high school, one was as likely to have a male teacher as a female teacher for any given subject, except gym and swimming. I never saw a male teacher in knickers or a female teacher in high heels.

As for hats, I saw two or three straw hats, worn primarily as conversation pieces. They had flat brims and low, oval, cylindrical crowns with flat tops; they were worn in summer. Visored caps (peak caps) were worn mostly by young boys and by those sporting knickers. But the hat of preference was the fedora, with its brim curled and its crown creased lengthwise. Many of the younger males uncurled the front part of the brim so that it drooped rakishly downward, resulting in a style called snap-brim. But, especially with the young, headgear was going out of style. In fact, everything seemed to be going out of style—well, everything *was*.

For example, I saw a horse-drawn fire wagon, a pumper, only once. But what an exciting sight it was! It came around the corner pulled by two big, galloping horses, and the boiler for the pumping unit was half-covered by its swirling steam vapor—low speed, but furious action!

Another imposing sight, but less dramatic, was the progress along the street of the big horse-drawn dray (cart for heavy-duty hauling) in the summertime or the huge sleigh pulled by mammoth horses in the wintertime. We children, who were always playing in the streets or the alleys, were warned of their coming by the jingle of the bells worn by the horses. As for the drays, we could hear the sounds of the approaching hooves and steel rims before we heard the bells, but the sleighs glided silently and were often almost on us before we heard their bells, since the fallen—and falling—snow muffled all sounds. We had narrow escapes.

Now the drivers of these vehicles, the teamsters, after passing my house would pull up at the saloon on the corner for a refresher. . . . What? A soft drink—are you crazy? Of course prohibition made the sale of alcoholic beverages illegal, but there was a loophole, an escape clause: beer with alcoholic content of 5 percent or less remained legal. Now that I think of it, many of those teamsters had the peculiar habit of drinking their beer out of whisky shot glasses— and so did policemen. The saloon was on the ground floor of a three-story brick building and occupied the long half of the ground floor, a length of about fifty feet.

As in so many corner buildings, the corner at the street intersection was cut at an angle of forty-five degrees for the entranceway, and as one entered (or, in my case, looked in) what met the eye was a large, long room with a high ceiling and a bare wood floor, empty of chairs or tables; there was only the long bar opposite the entrance. It extended the whole length of the room, and it was accompanied by a two-inch-diameter shiny tube, a brass rail that served as a footrest, supported six inches above the floor and under the overhang of the bar. Half a dozen shiny brass spittoons (cuspidors) were placed on the floor at intervals in front of the rail. The spittoons were shallowly filled with water for the tobacco chewers to spit into—and most of the teamsters chewed tobacco (. . . Look, if you spent most of your workday looking at the horses' asses, I think you'd chew tobacco, too.) The beverage, legal or not, could be accompanied by cubes of Limburger cheese, meat sandwiches, hard-boiled eggs, or other tidbits. The beer was a nickel a glass—a beer glass, that is—and the whiskey about fifteen cents to thirty-five cents a shot glass.

The postman would have mail for the saloon occasionally, especially on a hot summer afternoon, when he made it his last stop. The postmen wore gray uniforms and walked erect with military bearing (so did the policemen on their beats) as befitted respected public servants. They carried large, heavy brown leather bags by a shoulder strap, but they still radiated dignity. I felt sympathy for our mailman. As he passed our side door, he was from time to time assailed by the odor of tomato sauce being cooked for macaroni sauce, but it was a meat and tomato combination and included garlic, bay leaf, basil, parsley, olive oil, onion, and more. After two or three hours of simmering the sauce, raw or partially cooked meatballs were dropped into it for another hour or two of simmering. When breathed in, the vapors from the deliciously fragrant cooking sauce had the peculiar effect of making one weak in the knees. (. . . You're right. The odor of baking bread has that same effect on people who smell it. I have thought, at times, that humane wars would be possible if there were available bombs that carried the compressed vapors of baking bread or simmering macaroni sauce—southern Italian style, of course.)

But our postman faced other hazards—flying cats, for example. You see, my father was a cat lover of sorts. He would befriend stray cats with occasional feedings, and I'm sure that such cats passed the word along to their friends that, in case they were up against it sometime, my father was good for a handout. As a result, there was nothing unusual about the sight of a group of cats around our house, the individuals of the group varying with the time of day and the day of the week.

And we were seldom without a steady cat that had

access to the house so long as it conformed to two rules—well, one rule really; the other rule was optional and was the apparent cause, or at least one cause, for the frequent turnover of our resident cats.

(. . . I'm coming to the flying cat incidents, but I have to give you a little background first. . . . All right, all right. What's the hurry? You're not going anywhere.)

Of course, the very first thing a prospective resident cat had to learn was: never make dirty in the house. Such a thing happened only once per cat, because my father administered a prompt and completely effective lesson to the culprit. Upon discovery of the litter, usually by tracing the source of the odor, my father would immediately seek out the perpetrator, scouring the neighborhood if necessary. Seizing the cat by the nape of its neck, my father would carry it back to the scene of the crime and, holding its head about an inch above the smelly litter, lecture the cat in this wise (in Italian): "You see what you did? You make dirty in the house? This you don't do. No more. Only this once." It is doubtful that the cat understood the lecture, which, after all, was in a foreign language.

But the lesson was learned from what followed. My father would wipe the cat's head back and forth through the litter, firmly and thoroughly. One final wipe and the cat would be released to streak out of the house and to exercise one of its options: to never return or to show up when hungry and continue residency. My father never had a repeat offender.

I must stress that cats were much more independent in those days than they are today, mainly because food sources were plentiful for the stray. Almost every backyard had a woodpile, which rats appreciated, near the railroad tracks there were coal yards and lumberyards where cats and rats played a deadly hide-and-seek, and many backyards contained a chicken coop, which attracted not only rats but human predators as well. And then there were the usually open garbage cans where dogs, cats, and rats competed almost on a friendly basis because there was food aplenty for all. In fact, many house dogs and cats were seldom, if at all, fed formally in the house. Scraps were thrown to them outdoors, more to get rid of the scraps than to feed the animals. But from time to time, when pickings were lean, the animals would come around to the door for a formal meal. But if on such an occasion you had the poor judgment to suggest to one of the now-and-then cat visitors that you would appreciate more regularity in the timing of its visits, the cat (in our experience) would—I swear it!—sneer at you and stare at you with utter contempt. And in its wide-staring eyes you could read as clearly as though it were typewritten the insulting message: "Go fuck yourself!"

Yes, in those days, cats chased rats because there were so many rats around to chase, and dogs chased cats because, while the dogs were running loose between garbage can raids, it gave them something to do. However, there was one cat dogs did not chase. A hero cat. My heart swells with pride—honest—when I think of it. The cat—I'm ashamed to admit that I didn't even learn its name—belonged to an elderly neighbor, and because of its long fur it may not have been as big as it appeared to my eyes. Whenever charged by a dog, *any* dog, large or small, it calmly sat back on its haunches and raised its right arm straight up, claws extended, thus resembling a student with raised hand in a classroom. I always saw this spectacle from a standpoint behind the cat, since I would be in my backyard and the dogs charged in from the alley toward the cat.

One day, the charging dog turned out to be a very big German shepherd, much hated in the neighborhood because it not only chased cats but also killed those it caught, including pet cats. The dog seemed to enjoy trotting about with the killed cat dangling limply from its jaws. From my position behind the cat I witnessed the terrifying charge of the huge animal, and I expected that the intrepid cat would break and run this time. It's hard to say whether I or the dog was the more astounded. The cat did not budge, and the dog stopped six inches short of the feline and stared at it in utter disbelief—as did I. Can you conceive the courage of that cat to withstand such a charge and to stay eyeball-to-eyeball with a monster whose head alone equaled it in size? I think of Horatius at the bridge over the Tiber or David before Goliath.

At last, the German shepherd realized that this cat was not going to run. Still unsure of itself, the dog made an unwise decision to frighten the cat into running and to this end protruded its head toward the statuesque intended prey. The narrowed gap between the antagonists was closed by the cat with an action so swift as to be invisible. All I saw was the result: the formerly upright arm of the cat was now a gray horizontal bridge, a bascule bridge pivoted at the cat's shoulder and with its free end now firmly anchored in the dog's black nose by a rosette of stiletto claws. It was a brief spectacle, followed by a much more exhilarating scene for me—the sight of that mean hulk of a German shepherd retreating down the alley at a greyhound's pace. I sincerely wished to pay homage to that cat, but I was at a loss as to how to do so. In a negative sort of way, though, I managed. When I learned later that the same dog killed one neighborhood cat too many and that the dog was found dead of poison (presumably at the hand of an owner of one of the demised cats), I did not grieve for the dead dog.

Now the other rule a prospective resident cat had to learn was . . . (. . . What do you mean, what am I talking about? I told you there were two rules. The first rule was not to litter in the house. . . . Well, I interpolated the incident of the German shepherd and the hero cat. They were house cats. And they were house cats because they conformed to the two rules. I'm coming to that, but first let me give you rule two.)

Rule two for the house cat: all meals *table d'hote* (take it or leave it), no substituting. Cats learned rule two as follows. Upon refusing my father's proffered meal and opting to dine elsewhere, the applicant for house cat status was free to return at the next feeding time, when it would discover that not only had the menu not changed but the meal was the selfsame food that had been refused earlier. This experience usually resulted in the cat's sniffing unbelievingly at the contents of the food dish, raising and lowering its head in dismayed appraisal, circling the infamous receptacle while keeping a wary eye on it, and, finally, staring up fixedly into my father's eyes to relay its optical message: "Are you nuts? Get rid of this garbage and have something appetizing in this dish for the next feeding or get yourself another cat." And with tail high and one last contemptuous look, the cat would exit proudly.

At the next feeding time, when the cat arrived at the feeding dish it would behold in dumb amazement a plate full of pebbles. (. . . Pebbles. You know, little round rocks, that's all—no food.) It would just stand there gazing dully and—I probably imagined it—slowly shake its head from side to side as the realization came to it that "this guy is going to feed me what he cares to, whether I like it or not.

drawn to divide it into four triangles. In the centers of the triangles were the numbers 25, 50, 75, and 100. The householder placed the card in the window so that the uppermost triangle indicated the pounds of ice desired, and the iceman would take that amount of ice and deposit it in the ice compartment at the top of the householder's wooden icebox. Beneath the icebox was a pan to catch the water that flowed from the melting ice through a hole in the bottom of the ice compartment and into a tube draining down into the catch pan. Forgetting to empty the catch pan in time resulted in overflow onto the kitchen floor—and self-abusive language.

But it was at the commercial establishments where the iceman aroused admiration. I would watch his delivery at the grocery store that was two doors away from our house. First the iceman would enter the store and walk into the aisle between the counter and the big wooden icebox, which was seven feet high. He would open a stepladder in the aisle, ascend it, and slide aside the cover of the ice compartment; then it was out to the cart, where he draped a rubber sheet over his shoulder. Holding the ringed handles of the ice tongs in his hands, he would engage a block of ice (200 pounds, remember) with the two sharp points of the prongs and with a few tentative pulls make certain that he had a good hold and that the ice was firm. Then he would pull out the block partway, change hands on the tongs without losing his grip(!), bend his knees and twist around so that his back was to the cart, and pull the block onto his padded shoulder. Very carefully balancing, he straightened up. Now was the critical time. Another careful balancing and . . . he released one of the handles! From here on it was one hand only as he walked slowly across the sidewalk with that huge block of ice on his shoulder, up the two steps to the glass door that he opened with his free hand, down the aisle to the stepladder, which he ascended sideways and, reaching the appropriate step, shifting his footing and twisting his body so that his back was to the icebox. Then he let the block of ice slide back off his shoulder to land with a heavy thump in the ice compartment, the noise prompting the lookers-on to release their held breaths. All who watched were impressed, and I'm sure that the onlookers, like myself, felt like applauding this particular everyday task but felt too sheepish to do so.

But it was one of the residential icemen who, though not entertaining me directly, put me in the path of unexpected thrills. He would let me accompany him on his rounds occasionally and would assign me to collect from a customer who owed him money and who was not ordering ice that day, while he himself would be delivering ice to another customer nearby. I soon learned to brace myself for *anything* that might appear when a door opened to my knock: a nude woman, a man pointing a pistol at me, a frail woman barely managing to restrain a fearsome, snarling long-toothed dog ("he won't bite you"), a room apparently completely filled with furniture and other objects (there had to be a pathway somewhere), a very dark room with a darker silhouette of a person standing back from the person in the doorway, etc. I began to believe that though I might be terrified, I could not be really amazed at anything that might appear when a door swung open at my knock. But on mulling it over I conceded to myself that perhaps I could be amazed—and terrified—if what I saw was, say, a field artillery piece aimed at the open doorway or someone holding on a leash a baby hippopotamus.

As for the iceman himself, he did intrigue me with a story about a female customer of his who could not, or would not, pay him the five dollars and thirty cents she owed him. She readily agreed when he suggested that he "take it out in trade." After they returned from the bedroom, he announced to her that she had just reduced her debt by the amount of twenty-five cents. "What did she say to that?" I asked him.

"Nothing," he said. "It was all right with her."

I can dispose of the milkman and the fish peddler briefly so that I can get to the more interesting bread man and his horse. (. . . That's not so. I don't have a thing for horses. In fact, I dislike horses, or rather pictures of horses, and always have. I found that out early on in the barbershop. Just about every barbershop, if not every one, had a large, glossy poster calendar on the wall advertising some commercial product like a soft drink, say, or automotive parts. The poster almost invariably featured a next-to-nude beautiful woman either alone or with an animal companion, usually a cat or a dog or a horse. I strongly resented the horse. I don't know why, but I have since formulated a theory about it. However, I don't want to digress so, about the milkman . . . ? What's my theory? Are you sure? It's sort of raunchy. . . . You don't mind a little raunch now and then? Well, OK.)

I theorize thusly. Since time began, or maybe a little later, beauty in the form of a gorgeous woman has been coupled with unbeauty in the form of an animal and, more often than not, or at least as often as not, coupled sexually. For example, we have Eve and that snake in the tree, Europa carried off by a white bull, Leda and a swan, the lady and the golden ass of Apuleius' *Metamorphoses,* a queen and a unicorn, Beauty and the Beast, and a colossal ape with his captive heroine. Why this juxtaposition of a luscious damsel with a real or fancied animal? . . . Look; that was a rhetorical question. . . . I don't want to hear your theory. You asked to hear mine.... (Shut up! Now, where was I?)

Well, I assume all these animals were covers for gods or men, often outsize men, speaking genitally. And I could identify with all of them, except the horse. You had to admire their taste in women. But with a horse in the picture, I was out of it, and I can only put it down to jealousy. Yes, I was jealous of the horse and I think I know why. Whenever there was discussion with my companions about someone we knew who possessed outsize male genitals, we would remark that such person was "built like a horse." If such person being talked about was a black, it would be said that he was "heavy-hung" or "hung like a horse." It was the general consensus that all blacks were heavy-hung, and one of my brothers asserted positively that if he had to bet on which was the genitally bigger, a horse or a black man, he would bet on the black man every time. He believed that a hung jury consisted of twelve black men.

I may have internalized this association of a horse with a heavy-hung black man so that when I saw a poster calendar depicting a gorgeous scantily clad female standing there next to a horse I could not imagine myself as being the horse. The horse represented for me a black stud with whom I could not possible compete, since myth had it (and has it) that women prefer their male sexual partners with giant genitalia, if possible or if not, with enormous pudenda or, if not that, with horse-size privates or, failing that, at least heavy-hung, à la black men. And since on a scale of diminishing size, graduated in units down from ten, my penis would rate about a three (my jockstrap size is extra small) I resented the horse, which, subconsciously, I assumed was a stand-in for a heavy-hung black man, a ten. (Incidentally, God is rather heavy-hung, about an eight. I'll tell you about that later.) So there you have it. I would leave the barbershop somewhat dejected, and not even the cheery symbol of the barber trade hung outside raised my spirits.

Every barbershop had this paper cylinder, usually about six inches in diameter, on which were painted repeated sets of three spiral stripes, about an inch wide, one red, one white, and one blue. The cylinder was about four feet high, and it was enclosed in a clear glass cylinder that was attached to the shop front so that it cleared the sidewalk by about three feet. An electric motor rotated the paper cylinder slowly, with the effect that the colored helical stripes seemed to travel slowly and smoothly upward, with hypnotic effect on the steady viewer.

And that reminds me. Drugstores displayed their symbol, too—a real eye-catcher—not outside the shop like the barber's, but just inside the huge plate glass windows and on the extreme right and left of the window display areas. The symbol consisted of two parts, both transparent glass vessels filled with colored water and suspended by heavy chains to hang about two feet above the display floor, or about eye-level for a passer-by.

The one on the left (if memory serves me) was a sphere about eighteen inches in diameter and filled with red liquid; the one on the right was of comparable size and shaped like a child's toy, a spinning top, and filled with green liquid. They made a fascinating sight, especially at night with the lit interior of the store accentuating them. Incidentally, those drugstores sold only drugs. By the time they began selling ice cream, the symbols were gone.

Now, about the bread man and his horse ... (... Yes, I did say I'd discuss the milkman and the fish peddler first. All right, if you want to hold me to it.... It makes no difference to me. I just thought that since we were talking horses. . . . All right, I was talking horses, so I thought I'd complete the subject while I was on it. But to keep you happy I'll defer the bread man—and his horse. Let's talk about, or rather, let me tell you about the milkman.)

There is not much to say about the milkman except that he, too, was the subject of a myth. Since his delivery vehicle was not refrigerated and since most households did not possess insulated boxes to hold the bottles left by the milkman, the milkman started out very early in the morning, when the air temperature was at its coolest, and when possible he *ran* his route; otherwise he proceeded at the fastest possible walk. It was almost a nonstop operation; he spent the absolute minimum time in the vehicle, stacking his trays of empties and picking up his next customer's standing order. His route was one long hustle. One milkman told me that in delivering to apartment houses he found he had developed a sort of sixth sense for avoiding objects that were present in the dark hallways he raced through and objects left on the dark stairways he briskly ascended. He said that usually he could not see such objects, but he *felt* their presence and could avoid them almost without slowing his pace.

As for those stories about the housewife and the milkman, you can see now why they have to be myths. I never bothered getting estimated times from the perpetrators of coital "quickies," but logic tells me there is a bottom limit to the elapsed time necessary, starting from the meeting of the minds, continuing through the necessary divestment or, at least, rearrangement of clothing, and the duration of the act itself. The last, from my own experience, could be as little as half a minute. Let's say it is possible for the total elapsed time to be one minute. Now that's a quickie! But in a neighborhood like mine, with close-packed housing and with front door deliveries, the milkman could make two deliveries (of milk) in that one minute. Believe me, any liaisons between housewives and milkmen occurred outside his working hours. I hate to be a spoilsport, but it's iceman yes, milkman no.

On to the fish peddler. He was a weekly visitor to our neighborhood, which was constituted mainly of Roman Catholics (my family was the glaring exception), who religiously dined on fish on a Friday, so that each Thursday afternoon the air would be rent by a bugle call emanating from the corner of the block. It was the peddler's annunciation that he had fish for sale from his pushcart, the bottom of which was covered with chunked ice on which lay his varied piscine stock in trade (. . . Look; I just tend to talk that way. I get tired of plain everyday language sometimes. . . . No, I'm not trying to talk down to you. . . . What do you mean, it's not possible for me to talk down to you? Are you that intelligent? . . . Well, the same to you—and that goes double.)

Anyway, the peddler had a canvas stretched above the cart to ward off the sun, and he wore canvas gloves to handle some of the spiny-finned species of the erstwhile denizens of the aquatic depths or shallows. (You'll excuse my language, I hope.)

Soon the alerted housewives, those who were in the market, emerged from their houses and hastened to the fish cart, where they pointed out their choices; the peddler would place the selected fish on the pan of the spring scale at the rear of the cart and would announce the price. Upon paying, the housewife simply hooked a finger into the gill of the fish, lifted it off the pan, and walked home with it dangling from her hand. For the smaller fish, the housewife usually came prepared with a receptacle for carrying, but if she had neglected to do this, the peddler would wrap them in newspaper for her.

As the nearby trade dwindled, the peddler would move his cart partway down the block, stop, and again sound his bugle, a different call this time. In fact, as he proceeded down the block to the next corner and into the next block it became apparent to the interested listener that the fish peddler's taste in bugling was improvisation. Now generally improvisation in music moves me to a fury, but the fish peddler's bugle calls were so brief that they never breached my annoyance threshold and, in fact, I found them pleasant, in the way that a brief musical tinkling of bells is pleasant.

Now about the bread man—and his horse. . . . I'm glad you kept your mouth shut because, short as my arm is, your mouth is within my punching reach. . . . Go ahead; glare. You glare; I'll talk.) His customers, on our block, were all on the opposite side of the street because, by coincidence, the few non-Italian families on the block (German, Irish, and English) all lived on that side of the street, and they bought "American bread," that soft, white, spongy, air-filled, easily torn, and almost tasteless product that is still sold today. It has the happy property of becoming firm and tasty when it is toasted.

We Italians, of course, bought Italian bread, which was, and is, white, of heavy consistency, though spongy, and tasty (it's salted) whether toasted or not. It was called "curly bread" because of the curls formed when a rounded length of dough was bent alternately left and right to the desired width of the loaf to be baked, each bend being pressed closely to the previous one. This resulted in a loaf with a series of bumps on each side, the peaks of the bumps on one side lying opposite the valleys of the bumps on the other side. This construction had the advantage that the bread could be easily broken into equal pieces by hand if a knife wasn't handy, whereas "American bread" called for a sharp knife and a good eye to secure reasonably uniform slices. (Sliced bread was still years in the future, coming into vogue even after the strongly resisted canned food came onto the market.) Often, at the table, a loaf of Italian bread was passed from person to person, each tearing off one or more curls as desired if hungry or using a knife to even off the loaf and cutting slices, if hunger wasn't driving too hard and eye appeal could be given a chance to stimulate the appetite.

The bread man I am talking about delivered "American bread" and other baked goods from a horse-drawn bread wagon, which was high enough for him to stand in and had full-height openings in the middle of each side for his easy exit with standing orders for bread. The wagon was drawn by a tired old horse that seemed not able to lift its drooping head and moved with a heavily plodding slow motion. What amazed me about this horse was that it knew the houses of each of the bread man's customers, and I would watch with fascination the very efficient delivery of bread effected by this knowledgeable, slow horse and the nimble bread man.

Looking down the block toward the approaching bread wagon, I would see it come to a stop and see the bread man leap out of the opening in the curb side of the wagon and, with bread in hand, race up the walk leading to the front door of a house, and the moment the bread man's feet hit the ground the old horse would make a clumsy lunge forward to set the wagon in motion and then very leisurely pull the wagon along until it was opposite the front of the next customer's house, when the horse came to a stop and patiently waited for the bread man. If the bread man, as sometimes happened, had been able to make a very fast delivery, he could be seen emerging from the house and striding down the sidewalk while the horse and cart were still in motion, sometimes arriving at the next stop at the same time as the horse.

As for how the horse knew when the bread man had left the wagon, I guessed that the tilting of the wagon as the bread man stepped off resulted in some slight motion of the reins, which hung loosely at the front of the wagon, or perhaps the tilting caused some squeaking of the springs, or both. I don't think that the horse depended on the sound of the bread man's footsteps because, as I said, the horse made its move as soon as the bread man stepped off. As the bread wagon approached and passed by, I watched suspensefully, waiting to see at each stop if the horse had halted in front of the correct house. It always did, to my never-ending wonderment.

But I once had a much more intimate relation with an Italian bread man's horse. . . . (You know, I really appreciate your silence. Did you know that you are cute when you're silent? Now, now, don't blush.) I don't know how I got there, but there I was sitting next to the driver on the high seat of a buckboard, an open wagon with a canopy over the seat. The horse was pulling us at a trot southward on a busy street, through an area that was new to me, and I eagerly looked to the right and left as I craned my neck, in vain, to take in the passing scene. The trouble was that our seat put us only five feet from the horse's ass. I couldn't look over the horse's head as the driver could, and I couldn't look around it far enough to get a side view that was not changing at a pace too fast to absorb. It was like sitting in a theater where your view of the stage was almost totally blocked out by a tall person in the seat in front of you. I began getting very much annoyed at that horse. This led me to consider the situation of the driver, poor fellow, for his whole working day he had to be conscious in his view of the world of a horse's ass in the foreground. Surely, as the day wore on, this unending view of (in this instance) the north end of a horse going south must have increasingly irritated him, so that if, of an evening after work, he happened to be relaxing with a beer in some barroom and if, as is almost inevitable, he became engaged in an increasingly heated discussion with another beer drinker to the point that beads of angry perspiration appeared on his forehead, what is more natural than if and when his irritation defeated his self-restraint, he should bellow at his partner-in-conversation the epithetical judgment, "You horse's ass!"

Likely as not, above the long mirror on the wall at the back of such bar there would be a sign with an acronym on it. (. . . ? An acronym is the sequence of letters taken in order from the first letter, or first few letters, of each word of an expression. For example, take the expression, "*H*uman *L*ife *S*tatistics." The simplest acronym is *HLS*. Often it is desired that the acronym be pronounceable, so in this case *HULS* might be used. If the simplest acronym is pronounceable, it still may not be used because it may be embarrassing. For example, take the expression "*F*eral *A*nimal *R*esearch *T*echnology [FART]." The ones to which I refer, on the barroom wall, are the simplest acronyms.) Upon looking up after sipping, or guzzling, his beer, a customer might see on the barroom wall a sign bearing the letters "IITYWYBMAB." After unpuzzling his look and unwrinkling his brows, this customer likely would ask of the bartender the meaning of those letters, to which request the bartender would ask, "If I Tell You, Will You Buy Me A Beer?" One such customer—I won't tell you who—had to ask three times before he realized that the bartender had answered his question the first time and the second time and the third time. Some people just can't hold their beer, I guess.

But there was in vogue another acronym that represented another question, far removed intellectually from the one just cited. It posed a great paradox, one I still ponder from time to time. The acronym spelled *WIITTASMMHATTAH,* and it represented the paradox: "Why Is It That There Are So Many More Horses' Asses Than There Are Horses?" This paradox is yet to be resolved.

But, I digress. The horse lifted its tail, and while I was sitting there on that buckboard I was startled to see emerging from the horse's ass—well, emerging isn't the word. To me, *emerging* implies a relatively slow, smooth, and continuous development. Let's say I was startled to see extruded—no, extrusion also implies, I feel, a continuous expulsion (hey, maybe that's the word! No, I guess not, not quite); wait, I have it—ejected! I was startled to see ejected from the horse's ass a series of brown spheres about the size of a tennis ball. These, I found out later, are more elegantly referred to as horse droppings and somewhat less elegantly as horse balls; collectively, and vulgarly, they are referred to as horseshit. The ejections came at erratic intervals, some occurring singly and some in series of four, five, or six balls.

I noted, after recovering from my initial shock of surprise, that the horse balls were not homogeneous, there being evident on the surfaces what happened to be strands of straw. The balls broke easily into pieces when they hit the street, the horses' hooves, or the whiffletree, a bar pivoted on the wagon tongue and to which the harness traces were attached, thus enabling the wagon to be pulled. (There was an oft-sung song: "Oh, the old gray mare, she ain't what she used to be, ain't what she used to be, ain't what she used to be. The old gray mare, she ain't what she used to be, many long years ago. Many long years ago, many long years ago. The old gray mare she ain't what she use to be, many long years ago." There were many verses improvised and vulgarized, one beginning, "Oh, the old gray mare she [quarter rest] shit on the whiffletree . . . " etc.)

Considering the frangibility of the horse balls, I have concluded that their sphericity was made possible by the binding effect of the straw. Since the modern-type horse dates back to the Miocene epoch of the Cenozoic era, or about, let's say, 25 million years ago and modern human culture developed about, let's say, twelve thousand years ago, I would say that horses were making balls with straw a millionscore years before the Egyptians learned to make bricks with straw. I'd like to see somebody pooh-pooh that.

One more thing about horseshit—well, maybe two. The first thing finishes off my story of the buckboard incident. While the horse was still in the course of its anal ejections, I turned in my seat to view the long trail of droppings left in the street, and I saw something unexpected. Birds were swooping down and pecking at the broken horse balls, which apparently contained oat grains. (At this point I must warn you that I intend to begin a discussion of expressions both popular and vulgar, vulgar in the sense of crude, indecent, filthy, boorish, disgusting, foul-mouthed, etc. So you might want to cover your ears while you listen. And feel free not to interrupt, if you like.)

It was to be well over a decade later before I first heard the expression, "Aw, that's shit for the birds!" This exclamation from a listener signified that he placed no credence in what he had just heard said; and from a victim of some indignity, the outburst indicated that he resented being abused. I'd doubt that even one such expostulator in ten had any idea of the factual origin of the strained metaphor he had used unless he, like myself, had witnessed (or heard from hearsay) the actual event or situation referenced in the literal meaning of the expression.

Further, with distance in time and space from such event or situation, the facts tend to become less well remembered, variously remembered, and distorted (often deliberately). Also, there is the universal tendency to shorten words and phrases, which practice tends to make for abstraction of the original idea of the expression. Let me illustrate all this, starting with the basic, early expression:

> That's shit for the birds. (Even this is a shortening of "that's horseshit for the birds.") 1. What you just said is simply untrue. 2. That's grossly unfair. 3. (Euphemism) That's for the birds. My guess as to the mental gymnastics involved here: the repulsive lies are likened to horseshit, a gullible listener being the bird.
> Horseshit! 1. That's untrue! 2. (Alternates) That's a lot of horseshit; that's a lot of shit.
> Don't (try to) shit me. Don't (try to) lie to me.
> Don't give me that horseshit. Don't lie to me.
> Don't shit on me. Don't take advantage of me.
> Oh, shit! Shit! An expression of dismay or disgust.

It's evident from the example that the word *shit* in some of the expressions gives no hint that the excrement referred to is equine, not human. That fact alone illustrates how difficult it is for the curious to trace the origin and development of such expressions, especially since they are taboo, hence little studied in scholarly circles. (Remember that as I continue my very informal etymological appraisal of some few scatological expressions I have encountered. I wish you wouldn't wince like that. It's very distracting. I'll try to be brief.)

The first one is, "Your ass is sucking canal water." For the life of me, I can't get a clue on this one except in a negative way. I have never heard this expression outside New York State, so I gather it has something to do with the Erie Canal, for barges, which was built with mostly immigrant labor and was completed in 1825, cross-state from Albany to Buffalo. I can only *imagine* a scenario something like this: One of a barge crew falls into the canal, and as he is floundering there another bargeman, a coarse fellow, yells, "Hey, look at Joe! His ass is sucking canal water!" This expression may have caught on to signify, initially, derision of a clumsy person, later being perverted to its apparent present meaning: "You don't know what you're talking about!" That's the best I can do with that one.

This one's universal but even more mystifying as to origin and development: "You talk like a man with a paper asshole." It means "you are talking nonsense." Could it be descriptive of a gullible person who readily accepts anything he is told and mindlessly repeats it? That is, he readily takes it in (equated with easy anal penetration, or anal fragility, hence "paper asshole") and mindlessly repeats it, so he "talks like a man with a paper asshole." That's my best wild guess.

Here's another that is very widespread: "Go piss up a rope!" It's the equivalent of, "To hell with you!" I have a good imagination, but I'm at a complete loss at conjuring up an origin for this expression. Perhaps a circus roustabout urinated on a tent rope and tried to direct his stream upward.

And then there's, "Go pound salt up your ass," often

euphemized to, "Pound salt." For this one, there is perhaps a clue in the fact that salt is mined in New York State. I envision this scenario: Deep in a salt mine, the workers are busily breaking up salt deposits by means of jackhammers operated manually. An observer, noting the reciprocating motion transmitted to the operator's body by the jackhammer's pounding into the salt, would naturally correlate such motion with the pelvic thrusts of sexual intercourse, so that during an altercation in the mine, say, an exasperated salt miner might well be inspired to enjoin his adversary to, "Go pound salt up your ass!" in a refreshing variation of the classic, "Go fuck yourself."

Finally, we come to the universal classic and constantly employed, "Fuck you!" or, in the alternative, "Go fuck yourself!," over which I have often speculated. Of course, the obvious meaning is, again, "Go to hell!" And "Go to hell"—did I mention—signifies, "Go to hell and be consumed in fire, you dirty—,—,—,—bastard!" Fill in with adjectives, *ad libitum,* as many blanks as you desire.

The basic expression "fuck you" does *not* stand for the simple declarative sentence "I fuck you" or "I'll fuck you." Its meaning is "may you be fucked," and it signifies that rather than the utterer's wreaking calamity on you himself, he prefers to leave that action to someone else who may be so inclined. Also, the utterer apparently does not desire to have you die or be maimed or even bruised, but he does want you to be humiliated and more than just verbally abused, so he wishes that someone (else) will assault you sexually as a means of accomplishing for him the desired humiliation, inasmuch as he himself is not so disposed. Is that clear? (. . . What? Listen, you. . . . Listen, go. . . . Go—. . . All right, I'll calm down. But I want you to know that what set me off is that you used the expression before we discussed its etymology. I know that when you said, "Go fuck yourself," you were expressing disinclination to listen, or indifference to my exposition, but how is it you used a sentence with such a peculiar and seemingly unrelated literal meaning to express those ideas? . . . It's just the English language. You don't worry about it; you just use it? All right, just let me finish with the "fuck" expressions and I'll? . . . Yes, I'll quit fucking around.)

Now how do we get from "fuck you" to "go fuck yourself"? Apparently, there was no volunteer response to the utterer's general invitation to sexually abuse you, so in a confusion born of embarrassment he invited you to perform the act on yourself, never mind the difficulty. And when you pointed out the impossibility of carrying out his suggestion, he shamefacedly mumbled that he meant to say that you should masturbate yourself in public and so humiliate yourself.

However the expression stuck, and now "go fuck yourself" means "fuck you." Sometimes an imprecator will specify, "Fuck you in the ass!" or even, "Fuck you in the ear!" This latter startling suggestion may have a historical connection inasmuch as a legend has persisted since olden times in Europe that the Holy Spirit impregnated the Virgin Mary through her ear. Be that as it may, we also have the expression:

Fuck it.. 1. I don't care. 2. Forget it; ignore it; discontinue it. 3. I give up!

Fuck, be fucked (verb). 1. To cheat, thwart, or deprive someone. 2. To put someone at a disadvantage; to imperil someone. 3. To engage in penile-vaginal intercourse. 4. To press the penis against, or insert the penis in, any part of the body, e.g., to fuck in the ass, in the armpit, between the tits. 5. (Exclamatory) equivalent to, "To hell with—" e.g., Fuck the world!

Fuck (noun) An act of penile-vaginal intercourse (unless specified differently).

And: I'll be fucked if I do, will etc. I'll be damned if I do, will, etc. I don't give a fuck. I don't give a damn. Fuck off! Cease! Go away! Leave me alone!

Fuck-off (noun) Malingerer, avoider of responsibility or duty, unreliable person.

Fuck me! Not me (e.g., Fuck me, I won't go).

Fucking up: Making mistakes, doing it wrong.

Fucking off (military: fucking the dog). Idling, unbusy, relaxing, doing something that can be put off, malingering, avoiding work.

Get fucked! Same as fuck you, go fuck yourself.

Fucked up. Broken, inoperable, defective, confused (he's all fucked up), sabotaged, etc.

Some famous acronyms from the WW II era were:
- Snafu—Situation Normal, All Fucked Up
- Tarfu—Things Are Really Fucked Up
- Susfu—Situation Unchanged, Still Fucked Up
- Fubar—Fucked Up Beyond All Recognition

Fucking (noun). 1. Sexual intercourse (penile-vaginal, unless specified differently). 2. A setback, an abuse, a misfortune, etc., as in, "Boy, did I get a fucking!"

The words *fuck* and *fucking* (often corrupted to *fucken'*) are used prolifically as intensifiers, with *fuck* usually meaning "hell" and *fucking* usually meaning "goddamned," especially in questions:

Where the fuck is it?

Who the fuck says so?
Why the fuck should I?
What the fuck difference does it make?
When the fuck will you listen?
Where did I lay my fucking glasses?
Who gave you my fucken' phone number?
Why did you piss in my fucking yard?
What is the fucken' matter?
When did he file the fucking claim?
You're fucking right! You're fucking-A [letter A]! Right! Fucking-A!

And speaking of the word *fucking* used as an intensifier, I am reminded of a song that I have heard played and sung by Irish bands. The gist of the song is that someone holding a large bag enters a barroom and stands at the bar. Something is apparently moving about in the bag, and the holder reaches in, takes it out, and places it on the bar, whereupon the consternated bartender (and sometimes the customers, too) yells, "Get out of here with that— — — [three drumbeats] and don't come back no more!" When I first heard the song I knew what the missing words were: "Get out of here with that *fuck-ing thing* and don't come back no more!" To *my* consternation, no one to date has accepted my version of how to fill in the blanks. To me, it's so obvious! (. . . What, *chim-pan-zee*? Are you fucking crazy? A chimpanzee is three to five feet long. Never mind; let's drop it. No—wait, I'll give you another chance.)

I saw this old motion picture in which two men were having a serious altercation. They were about to sever their longtime association and had reached the stage of hurling invectives at each other. Finally, one of them headed for the door, opened it, and while holding the outside knob in one hand in preparation for a final grand slam of the door turned toward his erstwhile associate and vociferated, "Oh, yeah? Well, I've got only three little words to say to you!" And slam! Away he goes. Now, what were the unspoken three little words he was leaving behind as a sort of implied verbal defecation? (. . . "I hate you"? "I HATE YOU"? A furious, virile male shouts at another furious virile male. "I hate you"? You dumb bastard! . . . No, not "You dumb bastard"! Wait a minute—those *could* be the words. Appropriate, yes, but not likely the words 99,000 out of 100,000 average, raging, virile males would have used in that situation. By the way, how old are you? . . . That old and so naive? Now once again what are the three words almost certainly implied by the wrathful departer? . . . You do not know? I can't believe it. The "three little words" are, "Go fuck yourself." Now aren't you ashamed? . . . *Yourself* is not a little word? You mean you doubt that "Go fuck yourself" were the intended words? . . . Never mind. Just sit there. Relax; you'll be all right.)

3
Games, City Market

Perhaps you'd like me to discourse on some of the neighborhood games we children played. (You're nodding, aren't you? You're indicating yes, you'd like to hear aren't you? You're not sleepy? . . . (OK.) I'll just mention some you may have played when you were a "big kid," say around ten or more years old. Are you familiar with, run, sheep, run; kick the can; ring- a-levio? All these were elaborate variations of the simple hide-and-seek played by the little kids, but the players consisted of two teams and the area of play was an entire city block, the discovered hiders being "jailed" in a marked-off area from which they might be freed, by various means, by their uncaught teammates. When all the hiders were in jail at the same time, the rules were reversed so that the hiders became the seekers. As you might guess, it took hours to impound the entire team of hiders in the jail simultaneously, and sometimes night fell without the accomplishment of that task, so that the game would have to be continued the next day.

Of course, we played mumblety-peg (the tip of the blade of an open jackknife is touched to various parts of the body and flipped off with the intent of making the blade enter and stick in the ground) and many other games, most of them familiar to a broad spectrum of people, but there are two games we played that I am surprised to find are not known even to those people in the neighborhood who came as little as a generation behind me.

Did you ever hear of a game called nip? The dictionary gives as one meaning of the word *nip* "a piece pinched off, a small bit." So perhaps the game got its name from the five-or-six-inch piece of broomstick that was cut off and whittled to a cone on both ends to make what we called the nip. We cut off two more lengths of the broomstick, each being about two feet long, to use as striking pieces. As played by us kids, nip was a two-man (two-boy) game, though I see no reason why any number could not have played. The nip was laid down lengthways with the alley and then its cone—either end—was struck sharply with the striker. With a good strike, the nip would rise straight upward, rotating end-to-end meanwhile, a height of three feet or so, and the player then swung his striker to knock the nip as far away as he could toward a distant goal. As the players proceeded alternating, the one who drove his nip to the goal first was the winner.

It always intrigued me that the impingement of the cylindrical striker on the nip's cone resulted, when done right, in a vertical rise with end-to-end rotation of the nip. (Now, rather than being intrigued only with the motion itself, I am curious about the mathematical equations describing it. I could work the problem out, but I'm too lazy—I mean I'm disinclined—to spend time on a problem in kinetics when I could be daydreaming about what I would do if I won the lottery. I'm in no mood to attack a problem involving translation, rotation, center of gravity, moment of inertia, impulse, and momentum. But if you happen to feel like it and if you work out the nip equations of motion, I would appreciate your showing me your work.

I'll stake you to a triple-decker ice-cream cone. . . . I am not leering at you. . . . And I'm not being facetious. I gather from your comment that you aren't a physics major. . . . I did *not* know goddamn well that you didn't graduate from grade school, but even if I had, I wouldn't have abused you for it. Why, some of the most stupid people I know are college graduates. Besides, you should be flattered that I took you for one more educated than you are. Let me tell you about stick-in-the-mud. Tell you what; I owe you for one triple-decker ice-cream cone, OK?)

Another for-two game for kids—I can't recall whether we ever played three—was a very interesting and unusual one called stick-in-the-mud. For this game we needed a small bed of moist clay, which was no problem for us, since ongoing excavations for new houses were everywhere about. Alongside the alley we would make a roundish hole about one foot deep and about two feet wide, which we would fill with moist clay. Then each player would arm himself with a stick about eighteen inches long (usually it was a round stick), from the oak handle of an implement like a hoe, for example, so that it was heavy, strong, and of a size to fill the hand comfortably when grasped. If a heavy round stick was not available, then a square stick was used, one end being rounded for holding and one end of the stick pointed for driving it into the mud. So the dimensions of the sticks were arbitrary, they being chosen by each individual for the ease of holding and wielding, not too long, not too heavy, not too thin, not too thick.

Having by some means determined who went first, the loser threw his stick point down, of course, as deep as he could into the mud. Now the other player had three throws, if needed, to dislodge the first player's stick. The second player hurled his stick so that it struck a hard glancing blow yet bounced off at an angle that resulted in itself's being stuck in the mud. If that didn't happen, he lost his turn; the other player would pull out his stick and have his three tries. More often than not the second throw loosened the embedded stick sufficiently so that it could be dislodged on the third throw. The dislodger would then give the other player time to go off some distance of his choosing, say thirty feet, whereupon he would hold up or toss up the dislodged stick and knock it with his own stick as hard as he could toward the receiving player, who might try to intercept it even before it came to a stop. The dislodger then had to drive his stick into the mud three times before the receiver could arrive to drive *his* stick into the mud. If the dislodger succeeded, the game was repeated as before. But if the receiver was successful, he became the would-be dislodger. (Let's go get that ice cream I owe you; then I'll tell you of a couple of games the older boys or young men, the "big guys," played.)

There are other names for it, but we called our version of this type of leapfrog game huck a buck. It involved two teams of six "big guys," each with one team that, for convenience of this telling I'll call the frogs, and the other team I'll call the leapers. After choosing, by one of any number of ways, the losing team went first as the frogs. Someone not on a team would stand against a wall or pole or garage door, and the frogs would each bend at the waist in a line one behind the other, each with his shoulder against the rump of the one ahead of him (except the first frog, whose shoulder braced on the upright nonplayer), his head to one side and lowered and his arms around the legs of the person he was abutting. Thus one long back was formed of the six frog backs.

The leapers attempted to collapse the long-back formation by one after the other taking a running start and soaring through the air facedown as though making a flying tackle, landing as heavily as possible on the long back, each leaper trying to land as far up as possible to leave room for the leaper to follow. Usually the heaviest leaper led off, and since some of the big boys weighed about 180 pounds, the groans from the frogs began even before the lead leaper crashed down on them. Because of overlap, each succeeding leaper had to fly higher than the previous one and so he had to sacrifice distance. If the first leaper had not made a good long leap forward, the third leaper might end up just on, with the fourth leaper on his back and completely overlapping him; the fifth leaper would partially overlap the fourth, ending up almost vertical, his legs dangling, his arms around number four's waist; and number six would be forced to jump straight up to try to get his arms around number five's neck for support.

All this time the frogs' long back would be swaying and rippling as the frogs desperately fought the forces of the squirming mass on their backs, squirming because of bad landings or because of displacement caused by the frogs' movements to maintain balance. The landed leapers were not allowed to inch forward. Leapers would be hanging over the side, grimly trying to keep a foot from touching the ground and resulting in the leapers becoming frogs. If all the leapers were on and the frogs hadn't collapsed, the lead leaper would hold up one or more fingers and sing out, "Huck a buck, how many fingers up?" If the lead frog guessed incorrectly, play would resume with the frogs again being frogs; otherwise, with a correct guess, the roles would be reversed. And, of course, in the event of collapse of any part of the long back before the huck a buck call, frogs would be frogs. I should mention that this rough game was not played very often.

Mora (or morra) was played more often by the big guys, and as far as physical activity went, it was the antithesis of huck a buck, and except for dice or basketball, it was the group game of choice. It was a game of throwing fingers and was played in a garage to avoid the vehicular traffic of the alley, and it was played on sultry days, for a reason I shall disclose. An even number of players, usually ten, bought a case of beer, which was put on ice, and then they split into two teams of five players each. Then they went into an empty garage, leaving the doors open for light and ventilation, and each team formed a row, with the two rows facing each other man-to-man. The two opposing players of either end pair would play first, each looking the other closely in the eye as though fathoming how many fingers of one hand his opponent was likely to throw, none through five. The pair threw simultaneously, each shouting—and I mean shouting—what he guessed would be the total of his and his opponent's fingers thrown. And the shouting was always in Italian.

For example, one player might throw out his hand with one finger showing and shout, "Quattro. [four],"while his opponent, with two fingers showing, might yell, "Sei. [six]!" Since the total was three, neither would have won. Had both shouted, "tre [three]!," again neither would have won. But if only one of them had yelled, "Tre!" he would have won the throw, and as a reminder of his win, he would stick out the thumb of his nonthrowing hand. On his next win, he would also stick out his forefinger; thus the other players, and the onlookers, could see the score as play progressed. Five wins were necessary for a player to defeat his opponent. Then the next pairs played in turn until one team had the majority—three winning members.

And now the reasons for playing mora on a hot day became revealed: not only to enjoy cold beer, but also to torture some of the players. While the losing team stood fast, the winning team selected a "boss" and then its members resumed their same positions opposite the losers. And while all were standing there with perspiration beading on their skins, the boss allotted the beer, *according solely to his discretion,* to any of the players, winners or losers. An assistant boss was appointed by the boss, and he, too, could allot beer. So a loser could be quaffing sparkling cold beer while the winner opposite him slavered. Moreover, the boss or assistant boss might proffer a glass to a beerless player only to draw it back when the player reached for it, or keep asking a player if he would like a glass of beer but not respond to the acceptance of the offer, or spit in it and offer the glass. But even if the assistant boss wished to give a player some beer, he could not if the boss forbade it, usually ordering, "Don't give him any." Bitter enemies were made by the bosses in these games.

Since it was depression time, most of the young men were unemployed and so players were always available. The mora games often went on all day and the muffled shouts could be heard half a block away: "Tre! Sei! Quattro! Tutta la Mora!" *Dieci* (ten) was never shouted; it was always, "Tutta la mora [the whole mora]!" instead. (Tell you what; let's buy two beers and I'll play you mora for them. The loser is not to buy any more beer. . . . NO, no refreshment of any kind. Let's play in front of a hot stove. . . . You're right; that shows how old-fashioned I am. Where can you find a hot stove today? We could try the pressing room at a dry cleaner's. . . . OK, let's wait for a hot day.)

To be sure, the older men played games, too. Often they played cards for money and beer, but more often they played at bocce, a sort of bowling played on a long fine-gravel court laid out on someone's empty lot. The court was bordered with railroad ties to contain the balls, which might be rolled, bounced, or lofted full court. And these were not the regulation wooden bocce balls but four-inch steel balls that, I believe, were purchased through a sports store. First a smaller steel ball about two inches in diameter, the *pallino* (small ball), was thrown to the far end of the court; then the players of two teams would alternate throwing their balls, each player with the object of having one of his team's balls closest to the *pallino* after all balls had been thrown. Some spectacular throws were made when the *pallino* was blocked by two or three close balls to the detriment of the team of the player whose turn it was to throw. Since a ball rolled on gravel loses much of its momentum quickly and a bounced ball does likewise, it follows that the best way to scatter a cluster of two or three steel balls and a *pallino* is to hit the cluster with a ball hurled full court through the air. Some players were good at this and provided a fine show as they gauged the distance, assumed an olympic stance, and then fired the ball in a powerful low arc that ended in the crashing sounds of steel on steel, sparks, and the scattering of the cluster.

Twice, when the stakes were high, I saw played a novel variation of bocce. Instead of the gravel court, the paved alley was used from street to street, the whole length of the city block, which was about six hundred feet. Instead of four-inch balls, three-inch steel balls were used. The two teams stood at one of the intersections of the alley with the streets and rolled their balls toward the *pallino,* which had been propelled almost to the intersection of the alley with the next street. Very hard throws were required, and I still wonder that no child was injured of the many playing in the alley while the "bocce" game went on, the kids keeping their eyes peeled and avoiding the fast-rolling heavy steel balls. Since the ball-position situation at the *pallino* could not be determined from a block away, each team sent out a scout to shout back advice to the throwers. The stakes? Five dollars per player, too high for the players to enjoy the game; it was strictly for the money.

Let me give you an idea of how much food five dollars could buy at that time. The city market was four blocks from our house, and I would go there pulling a child's cart by the handle, or I would fold the handle back so that I could steer with it while I knelt with one leg in the cart and propelled it with the other till I arrived at the very busy marketplace. This was an area two city blocks long and almost a block wide, and vehicular access was by two streets bordering the long sides of the area. Down the long center of the area a wide raised sidewalk for the buyers stretched the entire two-block length, and on either side of the walkway were the farmers' vehicles, which they had backed in with their horses.

At one end of the walkway that intersected with a busy street was an eight-foot-high bronze water fountain for the horses, a very picturesque sight. Water rose in a column from the top, spread, and fell into an encircling and fancifully decorated trough, from which it spilled over in a circular sheet into four large basins in cloverleaf pattern at a convenient height for the horses to drink. The eye-filling sight of the fountain, the water sounds, the coolness of the water vapor that made the fountain area an island refuge from sweltering summer air—all against the background of the crowded marketplace and the busy street—provided an exciting experience for anyone, shopper, lounger, or passerby.

And even more hubbub was provided by various volunteers of my father's church who, once a month, sallied forth to the marketplace, formed a circle at the horse fountain, and, with the preacher at the center, sang hymns in Italian. Other church members who had come to shop would join the circle for a few songs, singing in English if they could and if the song happened to be a paraphrase of a familiar English hymn, and then go on about their shopping. On some other market night, a Salvation Army band might give a concert from on the sidewalk across the street from the marketplace. Directly across the street from the horse fountain lay a fabulous saloon, long bar, back mirror, sawdusted bare-wood floor, and all. A constant movement of farmers coming and going provided a pedestrian cross-stream to the heavy street traffic as they took advantage of what was, in effect, a farmer fountain.

What made the saloon fabulous was the copious and excellent food dispensed therein at no extra cost to the guzzlers: all the usual tasty bar nibbles and munchies, olives, hard-boiled eggs, cheese, cold cuts, but also hot foods such as bowls of fava beans with olive oil and excellent Italian sausage from the kitchen, which had a window opening at the end of the bar. Everyone wondered how the proprietor could afford to dispense such lavish free-with-purchase food. No one ever solved the mystery, but every customer relished it.

A farmer who had come to the market with no one to assist him would fight the clarion call of the canteen as long as he could and then, in the desperation born of his distress, engage any older boy of a shopping couple to stand in for him while he briefly lived it up in the big city. He would instruct the boy in the produce prices and turn over to him the cigar box containing loose change, and departing from his cares with only a vague reference as to how long he would be gone, it was off to food, drink, and comradery for him. His entrusted stand-in—notice I didn't say trusted, but what choice did he have?—would then sell the produce, making change as necessary and occasionally transferring some of the loose change from the cigar box into his pocket.

He did not concern himself with the patient horse on the opposite end of the wagon. It was tethered by its reins to a heavy, flat, round iron weight—it looked like a cow flop—that had a metal loop on top to which the loosely hanging reins were tied. And it was up to the farmer, at some time convenient to him, to loosen the reins, unhitch the horse, and lead it to the fountain to drink.

At that fountain I twice witnessed the literal truth of the adage "you can lead a horse to water, but you can't make him drink." It was no use for the farmer to pull the reluctant horse's head down by the reins to induce it to drink; the horse would shake its head from side to side and attempt to rear. It was to no avail for the farmer to explain to the horse that it was a long trip home and that thirst was likely to overcome it—the horse, that is—on the way home. The farmer made sure at the saloon that thirst would not overcome *him* on the way home, as he took on beer, whiskey, or beer and whiskey to last. And what about that dispensing of illegal whiskey? Well, with the Irish cops on the beat whiskey was considered simply the water of life; they believed in live and let live, and they took care to keep themselves alive.

(. . . Yes, I know; I know. I went to the market to

spend five dollars. All right, let's start from the fountain and proceed down the long, wide walk between the vendors on both sides.)

It was hard to see the produce for the people. One had to work his way slowly forward or to the sides where one confronted displays of fruits and vegetables that were of top quality, good quality, or, only occasionally, and in small amounts, slightly lesser quality. The farmers generally brought only the best of their products to market; I don't know what they did with their second-best. And since this was an age of large families and home canning, most produce was sold by the bushel; bushels of cherries, bushels of peppers, bushels of apples. . . . Sampling was permitted and invited. Plugs were cut out of watermelons on the purchaser's request, and I saw only one person who ever rejected a watermelon after tasting the plug—and that person was my father. When my father shook his head no, I happened to be looking at the farmer and noted with apprehension how the farmer's complexion began changing into deeper and deeper shades of red. I was greatly relieved when my father moved on.

Many kinds of live animals were sold for food, including ducks, rabbits, piglets, and of course chickens. Dressed animals were yet to come. Did you ever hear the expression "running around like a chicken with its head cut off"? I saw such a chicken more than once. Our neighbor had a tree stump in the middle of her backyard, which she used as an execution block for chickens she brought home from market. When her ax severed the chicken's head, she released the headless body of the chicken, which would run swiftly but erratically about the backyard for as long as five minutes, gradually slowing down before collapsing.

And when it came time for her two young daughters

to have their ears pierced for earrings, she used that same tree stump and an ice pick to perform the operations herself. It surprised me that the girls cried for hours afterward. I had assumed the pain would be minor and temporary, but the girls had tears in their eyes all day.

As for my mother's way with a chicken purchased at the market, she preferred to execute it by wringing the neck, then holding it over the sink and cutting its throat with a kitchen knife. It took considerable force to cut through the neck feathers to open the throat and hold the squirming chicken while it bled into the sink. The sight revolted me.

Well, just let me say that when we returned from market the child's cart would be bearing a load of the finest produce piled into as high a cone as possible, any excess being carried by hand, and all for five dollars. Chickens were grasped by the feet, and they hung swinging to the holder's walking cadence. Now you can appreciate why playing alley bocce for five-dollar stakes was a serious business.

If you'll allow me, I'd like to mention one more sport before I go on to sex. (Suddenly you're alert, chin up, eyes sparkling! Can it be that you are still that interested in sex. . . . Sex a sport? You're not a practicing Catholic, it would seem. Let's not debate the point. I am not going to moralize; I'll simply relate some of my sexual experiences.)

Some of the larger drinking places, called inns or barrooms or bars (the word *saloon* was becoming little used), held dances on Friday and Saturday nights and provided tenpin bowling in the basement, where there might be one, two, or three alleys. Few customers bowled for the sake of sport, the activity being indulged in merely as an aside to the drinking and dancing upstairs. But pin boys retained by the management would appear, or be found, to set pins, which were shaped like Indian clubs and fifteen inches high, for the occasional bowlers who descended the basement stairs. The pin boy, also called pin setter, would turn on the lights over the alley to be used, walk down one the gutters alongside the alley to his pit at the back, and, picking up the loose pins, if any, from the pit floor, place them in the rack, situated some two feet above the end of the alley. Then, by means of a handle on the rack mechanism, he would pull down the rack and hold it down until the pins, which had slid through holes to an upright position, stopped wobbling. Releasing his pressure on the handle allowed the rack to return to its raised position, leaving each of the pins set on one of the ten spots in a triangular array on the alley. Some of the older boys had worked at setting pins before the advent of the racks, placing pins individually and by hand on the spots. Those boys were called pin spotters, and their activity was called spotting pins.

Once the pins were set, the pin boy hopped up to a padded shelf attached to the back wall and drew up his legs to escape the flying pins to come. From this vantage point he could look over the rack and see the bowler select a ball from the ball rack, which was the final portion of the elevated ball-return raceways extending from the pits to the players' area. The balls were wooden, had either two or three finger holes drilled in them, and were a little over eight and one half inches in diameter and weighed sixteen pounds. The pin boy then saw the bowler back away from the starting line, called the foul line, so as to get a running start and then run forward up to the foul line swinging the ball forward and bending his body so as to deposit the ball onto the alley with as little bounce as possible, taking care that no part of his body touched the alley beyond the foul line through overstepping, skidding, or losing balance.

Now the pin boy saw the ball rolling swiftly toward him along the wooden alley, either in a straight line or in a curve, and if it did not drop first into one of the gutters on either side of the alley it would smash into the triangle of pins, knocking either all or some of them down. Some pins would fly or roll into the pit, some into the gutter(s), and some would roll to a stop on the alley. At this point the pin boy would jump down from his perch, transfer the ball from the pit floor to the ball return, and clear the alley and gutters of the fallen pins, placing them in the rack above the empty positions on the alley. If the bowler had not made a "strike" by knocking down all the pins, he was entitled to throw one more ball at the remaining pin(s).

Once in a while a very powerful bowler would strike terror in a pin boy by propelling the ball with such great force as to cause the flying pins to reach the pin boy on his perch. This type of problem was of short duration, because the pin boys would refuse to set pins unless the bowler would throw with less force or the bowler would try throwing with less force and find that he played less well or that his enjoyment was diminished by the enforced restraint and quit bowling.

However, I went into a little detail about the game so that you might better appreciate the story I'd like to tell you about a certain female bowler. Occasionally women would accompany their male escorts down the basement stairs to try their hand at bowling, and a few did so often enough to become fair bowlers. One of these latter had a peculiar talent in that she scored well through throwing a very slow ball, which seemed to take forever arriving at the pins. I should mention that the distance from the foul line to the "one pin," the pin at the corner of the triangle closest to the bowler, was sixty feet; the alley was forty-two inches wide. She threw a very slow ball, but she threw with remarkable control, and all present liked to watch the slow-motion drama as the languid ball proceeded with a low rumbling sound to close the long gap between it and the triangular cluster, finally arriving and accurately entering the array along a line between the one pin and the two pin. (She was a left-handed thrower; right-handed throwers aim for the opening between the one pin and the three pin.)

With the arrival of the barely moving ball, the pins began an almost balletlike spectacle, slowly tipping and contacting adjacent pins with a series of *plic!-plic!-plic!* sounds and then sliding along each other to fall so lightly that some pins rolled very little and some not at all. Most of the fallen pins remained on the alley rather than rolling into the pit or the gutters. On three different occasions, I saw here bring down nine of the pins with her first ball, leaving only the seven pin standing. And those were occasions for a different spectacle produced by this bowler.

I must explain that the seven pin is the one on the left back corner, as viewed by the bowler, of the triangular array of pins. To hit the lone seven pin with his second throw, a bowler throws from the right side of the alley and diagonally across, so as to keep the ball away from the left gutter in the event the ball's course tends somewhat to the left of the seven pin. But this particular woman— she was left-handed, remember—laid the ball down (at least she seemed to lay the ball down rather than propel it forward) on the left edge of the alley so that almost half of the ball hung over the gutter. And in that fashion the ball proceeded at an agonizingly slow pace along the very edge of the gutter until with a little *plic!* it nudged the seven pin before it went into the pit. Slow-motion magic. As I said, I saw her do it on three occasions. I'd like to see a professional bowler "pick up" the seven in that way, or the ten pin if he's a right-hander.

4
Early Sex, Personality, Fermat's Theorem

And now for the pièce de résistance, my discourse on how sex encountered me and how I encountered it. I shall pursue this discussion with resolve, persisting despite the nature of my various experiences, whether or not titillating, moral, legal, prurient, disgusting, varisexual, uplifting, or in or out of the norm, and even if I come face to face, so to speak, with an occasional vulva I shall not turn away. I . . . (. . . Enough of litany, you say? Nay, this is but prologue, but I accede to your impatience, sirrah, and will have done with it. List, then, and hearken well to my recount, nor be churlish with interruption, nor dour of mien if my disquisition suit thee not. Ahem!)

My earliest sexual experience occurred at about age three. To describe it, I take my mind to a level lower than the gutter, because it happened in the basement of a neighbor's house. A group of grown boys and girls were playing a form of blind man's buff that they called blind man's bluff. They formed a circle in the center of which stood a blindfolded girl who was attempting to touch any one of the group who were calling teasingly at her, approaching softly, and gently pushing her or running very closely past her. She was a rather plumpish, pretty, and good-natured girl, and I liked her very much. She kept turning, taking short steps and thrusting out her arms so that when, as small children tend to do, I wandered into the group of people, her reaching hand touched me.

Immediately she tore off her blindfold and gazed in surprise at her catch. Then, swiftly recovering, she held me by the shoulders and kissed me full on the lips. I was amazed at the softness, the warmth, and the sweetness of her lips, and I felt a delicious glow that quickly suffused my whole body and caused me to go limp. The thought of it now, and whenever I happen to think of it, gives me a glow of quiet pleasure. (How's that for a start?)

About a year or so later, a group of preschoolers, I among them, was playing in the alley while close by in a neighbor's backyard a group of preschool girls was playing house. One of the little girls wore nothing under her dress, and so her uninhibited activity resulted in frequent flashes, or sometimes stills of her ... her ... well, it was an oval prominence at the juncture of the insides of her thighs with her torso; it looked like a chicken egg, extra large, with a vertical and central fissure extending from tip to tip. Of course, all of us boys had seen these on our baby sisters, but the chance sight of one of these on a three-year-old had a curious effect on the boys: they tittered (... yes, tittered) and stole embarrassed sidewise glances at it and at each other. I wondered at this behavior, since I was inclined to gaze calmly and frontally at the oval medallion. After a brief interval, and with a little reluctance, we returned to our play and ignored the girls.

So there was an early indication, had I only recognized it, that I was a person more cerebral than emotional, more inclined to view critically than to wait for or accept a majority reaction. I did not realize then that I have this infirmity: I try to reason with people. Due to the long inattention span of the average human, this reasoning can only be done in a formal setting (speech, book, broadcast, etc.) where an audience can't talk back, so that by emphatic repetition and suitable examples the reasoner can hope to catch some of those random, fleeting "on" moments in the consciousness of his audience. I . . . (. . . Who's philosophizing? I am merely indicating that because of my propensity to reason, I was to endure a lifetime of being in the minority, sympathizing with the underdog, questioning inept authority, resenting injustice, urging cooperative thinking and acting, and attempting the ultimate in futility: getting people to lift a finger in their own defense. . . . The other boys? No, I would not classify them as emotional. For me, that is a secondary characteristic of humans; I classify them in three primary categories: thinkers, observers, and actors, all of whom are more or less emotional.)

I'm a compulsive thinker and, as a consequence, a very poor observer and a hesitant actor. Observers fascinate me as they constantly peer and scan, searching primarily for any sign of motion, in which respect they act for all the world like dogs. In their constant searching they often observe interesting stationary things that, when they apprise me of them, seem so obvious that I cannot conceive how they escaped my attention. However, not seeing obvious stationary things is a universal failing. (None of the stereotypes is pure, of course. Thinkers observe and act, observers think and act, and actors think and observe. I classify them by which they seem to be primarily.)

As a good example of not "seeing" the obvious even as you look at it, I cite the large sycamore tree at the corner of my block. From its size, I would judge that it is much older than I am. I have been turning that corner at least three hundred times a year for these many decades, passing that spectacular tree standing four stories high with its bark displaying multicolored blotches in browns, yellows, grays, and off-whites as though it were a clown's costume, yet I "saw" it only two years ago, to my utter astonishment.

Here's another example, from a nonthinker—I'm sorry, from an observer type. It so happened that I had purchased a book on the history of architecture and had lingered on the discussion of cornices, which line the tops of mostly older buildings and which project beyond the walls in the form of a decorative horizontal moulding. In olden times, the cornices were supported by the ends of beams projecting through the walls and the beams' ends themselves were often ornamentally carved, one common type of carving resulting in a beam end that put a viewer in mind of a bird with a large beak nesting under the cornice and so coming to be called a corbel, meaning a little raven.

Most old commercial buildings have decorative brackets imitating, and called, corbels under the cornices; all you have to do is look up to see them—I mean to "see" them. That's what I did after I had read the discussion in the book. From outside my house I looked across several backyards to the three-story red brick building half a block away and flanking the far side of the street, and there, for the first time, I "saw" a splendid row of corbels under the cornice, brackets in the classical, nesting "crow" shape, spaced about eighteen inches apart for the entire length of the building.

A few days later I was talking over the fence to a neighbor about my new awareness of architectural details on houses and other buildings. He was facing the building as I had a few days earlier, and as I rounded off my little lecture with a discussion of corbels, I pointed to the building and I ended, "... like the corbels on that building." He cried out in amazement, "I never saw those!" Yet there were few days in his life when that building had not been in his sight. He, even as I, had just never bothered to "look" at it.

(... What's the upshot of all this? The upshot is if even an observer type can be so unaware of his surroundings, think of how much more the thinker and the actor are unaware, especially the thinker. At least the actor tends willingly to stay fairly alert for hazards as he moves, whereas the thinker—unless he's, say, driving a car, and even then—has to struggle unwillingly to suppress thought in order to observe his surroundings, if only for safety's sake. You can see how your stereotype will likely affect your attitudes, reactions, values or lack of values, schoolwork, job, love, life ...... Godammit, I'm not philosophizing! I'm just imparting an appreciation mostly of how—very little of why—life and I reacted with each other. I realize that "why?" is almost impossible to answer, so I'm steering clear of it. I stated as a *fact* that, given a choice, I prefer thinking to observing or acting my way through life, though I mix it up somewhat. Now, may I proceed?)

For the third stereotype, the actor, I give as example a person who was a young man when I was a youth. He was unemployed and had a sports car with a rumble seat and an abundance of nervous energy. Standing beside his car, which was parked at the curb, and jingling the loose change in his pocket as we talked, he stated, apparently on the spur of the moment, "I think I'll go to New York City for a few days. What's the best way to go?" He meant, "What's the best route to follow?" I certainly didn't know, but I suggested that he go to a gasoline station for a road map. He dismissed that suggestion as a waste of time; instead he stopped a stranger walking by on the sidewalk and asked him the same question. The stranger thought a while, then gave him some route numbers sufficient, if followed, to get him out of town and headed in the general direction of New York City. That was good enough for the actor. He jumped into the car, brought it to life, and was careening around the corner before the stranger had moved on twenty feet.

Apparently, the actor was accountable to no one. Perhaps not, but I have encountered that type often. And often, I have found, their apparent spontaneous actions are premeditated and well planned. They may be romantic and enjoy startling people, or they may be perverse and enjoy asking for an opinion or information so that they can ignore it or act oppositely to the recommendation, to the discomfiture of the person trying to be helpful. If they act in such manner frequently, they are simply labeled as nuts; if not too frequently, kinda nutty. But, of course, this was an extreme example. Active people think and plan but tend not to spend *too* much time on it.

(By the way, speaking as a thinking person, did I tell you about my solution for Fermat's Last Theorem? . . . You have no idea what I'm talking about? . . . And you don't care to know. What if I told you that in the year 1908 a prize then worth about $1 million was offered for a solution? The prize still exists but is now worth only about sixty-six hundred dollars because of inflationary and other financial changes. So, in more than three hundred years (Fermat flourished in the mid–seventeenth century) no one has produced an accepted solution.)

. . . ? Well, yes. Like thousands and thousands before me. Would you like to hear it? . . . You might, if you knew what it's all about? Basically, it's about triangles, right triangles of a special kind called Pythagorean after a mathematician of the sixth century B.C. . . . You don't know anything about math? Great! Then you won't be able to point to a fallacy in my proof. I can proceed with confidence.

Of course you know that one of the three corners of a right triangle is square [the sides are perpendicular to each other] and is called a right angle and Pythagoras is credited with proving that any such right-angled triangle, called a right triangle for short, has the peculiar property that the longest side multiplied by itself equals the sum of both shorter sides multiplied by themselves and then added together.

. . . Of course you're confused. Here, let me draw you a picture of a right triangle. . . . Watch out, clumsy! You almost knocked over my glass. Call the longest side, the one opposite the right angle, Z. Call one of the shorter sides X and the other one Y. Now, as Pythagoras proved, we can say that:

Z times $Z = X$ times X plus Y times Y, or $Z \times Z = X \times X + Y \times Y$, which we can rewrite as $Z^2 = X^2 + Y^2$, for short. OK so far?

. . . All right, I'll use numbers for an example. Since X and Y can be any two numbers, except zero of course, let's say X is 3 and Y is 4 so that: Z^2 ($Z \times Z$) = 3^2 (3 x 3) + 4^2 (4 x 4). Now let's figure out how much Z is. How much 3 x 3? . . . I said, "How much is 3 x 3?" . . . You're figuring it out? It's 9. Stop fooling around. Now how much is 4 x 4? Never mind; it's 16, so Z^2 = 9 + 16, or 25. What's Z? . . . What number multiplied by itself gives 25? . . . Good guess. Five. So $5^2 = 3^2 + 4^2$ is a particular example of *all* the right triangles possible, as represented by the general formula $Z^2 = X^2 + Y^2$. Just make X and Y any two nonzero numbers and you can find Z, the longest side of the right triangle, by applying the formula as we just did.

... Your head is starting to hurt? Just be patient and pay attention. How would you like a piece of the prize if my solution to Fermat's Last Theorem is accepted? ... How big a piece? A bottle of whiskey, deal? ... OK. I have to point one thing out before proceeding with my proof. If you double *each* side of a triangle, you get a triangle of *the same shape* but twice as big, called a similar triangle to the original. And if you triple *each* side of the original triangle, you get a similar triangle three times as big. Generalizing, if you multiply *each* side of a triangle by any number, call it a, you get a similar triangle a times as big. In other words:

$Z^2 = X^2 + Y^2$ (original triangle with sides Z, X, Y)
$(2Z)^2 = (2X)^2 + (2Y)^2$ (similar triangle twice as big)
$(3Z)^2 = (3X)^2 + (3Y)^2$ (similar triangle three times as big)
$(aZ)^2 = (aX)^2 + (aY)^2$ (similar triangle a times as big)

Now don't forget, *each* of Z, X, and Y must be multiplied by the *same* number in order to get a similar triangle (same shape) as a result. Let's have a short drink.

Now for the proof. ... What do you mean, proof of what? Fermat's Last Theorem, as I said. ... What is it? Oh, yes. Well, Fermat said that although you can have solutions to $Z^2 = X^2 + Y^2$, where Z, X, and Y are whole numbers (not fractions), as in the 3, 4, 5 triangle we talked about, you can't have solutions to $Z^3 = X^3 + Y^3$ (Z x Z x Z = X x X x X + Y x Y x Y) where Z, X, and Y are whole numbers. In fact, he said there are no solutions to $Z^n = X^n + Y^n$ where n is any whole number except 2, with Z, X, and Y also being whole numbers.

So let's see; we have

1. $Z^n = X^n + Y^n$ (Z, X, Y, and n all whole numbers)
$Z^{\frac{n}{2} \times 2} = X^{\frac{n}{2} \times 2} + Y^{\frac{n}{2} \times 2}$ (multiplying by 2/2 = 1 changes nothing)
$(Z^{\frac{n}{2}})^2 = (X^{\frac{n}{2}})^2 + (Y^{\frac{n}{2}})^2$ (form of a right triangle)

or

2. $(Z \times Z^{\frac{n}{2}-1})^2 = X \times X^{\frac{n}{2}-1})^2 + (Y \times Y^{\frac{n}{2}-1})^2$ (right triangles)

or

3. $(Z)^2 = (X)^2 + (Y)^2$ (right triangles)

And if any solution of 2 is a triangle whose sides are all whole numbers, then that triangle must be similar to one of the triangles of 3, because three contains all possible whole number (Pythagorean) triangles. Do you follow me? . . . Do you follow me? Put that glass down! Stop nodding!

But 2 cannot be similar to 3, because Z, X, Y in 3 are *not* each multiplied by the *same* number in 2. So 2 can have no whole number solutions—except when $n=2$, because when $n=2$, 2 becomes the same as 3. And if 2 has no integral solution (except when $n=2$), then 1 has no integral solution (except when $n=2$) because 2 is just a different form of 1. Q.E.P. There, what do you think of that? . . .

You liked the part about the similar triangles? Thanks. . . . *Q.E.P.* means "which was to be proved." Well, did you find any fallacy in my proof? . . . No? I'm greatly relieved. Do you think I should apply for the prize? . . . You really like your whiskey, don't you?

Well, time, which is forever passing, kept at it for another two years, until I was about seven or eight, which is when I got a traumatic introduction to the adult female genitalia. Strictly speaking, that's only partially true because, though I had a clear shot at it, I could only see part of it because the light conditions weren't that good and besides . . . (. . . Quit beating about the bush? Hey, that's good! Ha, ha!) Anyway, it happened in our kitchen. One of the neighbor girls, in her twenties, trim, blond, pretty, pleasantly dispositioned, and very likable, was seated in the middle of the kitchen and wildly dangling my baby brother on her knee. It was a warm day, and she seemed to have little clothing or none under her dress. Each time she raised her knee with my brother on it a long length of bare thigh was exposed to my view from in front of and a little to the side of her. I kept bending lower and lower to see more and more of that gleaming thigh, and finally she noticed what I was doing. I noticed her hesitation as she considered how to react.

Then, with the suggestion of a toss of her head, that darling girl raised my brother high and held him there, and furthermore, she spread her legs. Except for her shoes, she was bare to the waist, and holding her position, she shook my baby brother gently and cooed at him while looking at me out of the corner of her eye. And I looked at her in utter astonishment. I could not absorb the sight. Apparently, subconsciously I had been prepared to discover something resembling a cracked ostrich egg, a large, smooth white oval riven centrally and vertically with a tip-to-tip canal. What I saw was a large tangle of *blackish* hair that looked for all the world like a carelessly made bird's nest. But . . . hair! And so much of it! Nothing else was visible. I took a long, long look with wide, wide eyes while she kept my baby brother aloft, until I finally turned away, figuratively shaking my head at the strangeness of it all. It was to be a long time before I got to see beyond the hair barrier (not hers, a different one).

While we're on the subject, I must say that I find some of the names for the female genitalia not suitably descriptive. For example, monkey. In no way does a woman's pubic hair resemble a monkey or put a person(a sober person, anyway) in mind of a monkey. The same goes for beaver, which name is more frequently used than monkey. And the same goes for pussy, the slang name most often used for the purpose. The only connection that I can surmise between these animal names and the hair surrounding the vulva is that the woman's hair envelops something alive and warm and fur does the same for an animal. Hence, I surmise further, we have the excellently descriptive but seldom-used muff. In fact, muff is used almost exclusively in the expression *muff diver,* which signifies a person who engages in cunnilingus, which is polite for the universal and constantly used cunt lapper.

But the best descriptive name for it, surpassing muff in this respect, is hardly ever used outside literature, and that name is William Shakespeare's: nest. For a bird's nest is exactly what appears to be lodged between the females lower limbs at their junction with the trunk. True, some of the nests are more tidily made than others (the one I saw was slapdash), but nonetheless, all are so like a bird's nest that a bird overflying a nude female sunbather might well consider laying an egg in such a nest. Honest. I mean it.

No use letting go of the subject now. Other words used for the female genitalia go to greater depth. Take, for instance, *nooky,* which I construe as a little nook, and a nook is a small recess. Another structural name is the self-defining gash. (The big guys would say, "Let's go gashing," rather than, "let's go look for girls.") There's also box. A functional name is snatch; an operational name is squish; and a gustatory name is hair pie (for the muff diver.)

5
Automobiles, Streetcars, Entertainments, Puzzles

In its inexorable way, time continued to elapse, gradually electric lights got brighter, automobiles more numerous, radios more static-free. Prohibition enforcement raids were frequent enough for me to witness some of them in progress. Whenever the fire trucks pulled up a block or two away and no rising smoke was evident, the gathering crowd would see the firemen entering a garage whose doors were open wide and from which issued crashing sounds. A look through the open doors would reveal that the wooden garage floor had been a false one that the firemen had removed, leaving exposed the room below, which was filled with whiskey-distilling apparatus and large glass bottles, each capable of holding at least twenty gallons of liquor. The crashing sounds were produced by the firemen down there who were smashing the distilling equipment and the bottles with their axes. Who tipped off the authorities, a neighbor? Or a competing clandestine distiller in the next block—or in the *same* block?

Of course that other ubiquitous, sinful, and unlawful activity, coeval with hard drinking all during human evolution, that is to say prostitution, also flourished in our city, and once I witnessed a poignant incident related to the white-slave traffic. It was late on a warm summer night, midnight, and I was sitting on the curb in front of the house, idling. School was out, so my mother allowed me to choose my own bedtime. The scene was lit by the streetlight on a pole two doors down from my house. As a big automobile approached from the side opposite the streetlight, I was struck by its very slow movement, so I arose from the curb and stepped back to the sidewalk to watch it. The interior was dark and the passenger half of the windshield was shuttered!

As the car drew abreast, I was astonished at the size of it. It was not just big; it was huge. The motor, no doubt had sixteen cylinders, since it ran so quietly. It was a tan color and, to my amazement, had tan shades drawn down on every window.

Just as it passed me, it came to a sudden stop. I heard a woman's weak cry, which was cut off immediately. Then the car started up and proceeded down the street at the same slow pace as before. To me it seemed certain that a woman was being kidnaped into the white-slave trade. I wanted to telephone the police, but we had no telephone. The grocery store opposite the streetlight had a telephone, but the store, as usual, was closed at midnight. There was nothing I could do. I just stood there. That pathetic choked-off cry, that tragic scene—they still visit my memory from time to time.

About those sixteen-cylinder cars, they ran so quietly that their engines could not be heard idling even if one were standing, as I found myself standing once, next to the hood of one of these giants parked at the curb. I knew that the engine was running, so out of curiosity I put my ear to the hood, and I still could not hear an engine noise. In a way, such cars were scary in that if you were standing near the curb and not observant of them, they could come right up to you unawares. In this respect they were startling and dangerous. All the cars at the time were big or small. The small ones were the new cars for ordinary people. Gradually, newer and larger types of cars began to supplant the smaller ones and the number of cylinders per car would increase from four to six to eight while at the same time the twelve-cylinder and sixteen-cylinder cars began to disappear.

But most people walked to their destinations or, if near the trolley line, rode on the trolley car for ten cents. The trolley car ran on rails down the center of the street and got its electric power from the wire to the trolley wheel which rolled along the power line above the street. The trolley cars were open-sided and had pairs of facing wooden benches along both sides of the center aisle. Several floor-to-ceiling metal poles were distributed along the outside edge on both sides of the car for grasping to swing aboard, for these cars did not stop till the end of the line. They rolled slowly along and you pursued them with a slow run, or you intercepted them in a walk if you were close enough. I never heard of a boarding accident, though there must have been some.

And where would the trolley cars take people? Well, to the main shopping districts and to the "shows," as we called the motion picture palaces. The big shows really were palatial, but all the motion picture theaters, down to the smallest, were as ornate as the proprietors could afford. Only one I attended had a plain interior. It was the smallest of them all, and the first few times I attended (admission: three cents) it was running silent films. Alternately, the actors would be seen moving their bodies and lips, then the scene would be replaced with the words they had just silently said, in white letters on a black background. Since I could not read yet, I would close my eyes when the words came on and try to time their opening with the resumption of the picture. Meanwhile, a man playing a piano located below the screen kept music going.

Most of the main features at this time were cowboy pictures, with a few comedies and pictures of World War I mixed in. Occasionally the hero of the cowboy silent picture, the "good guy," would do something very out of character: he would swear. Yes, he would. He would become very, very angry with the villain, the "bad guy," and curse. This oath, the only profanity permitted a good guy, was *son of a bitch*. Usually the hero would be in a fix in the middle of the desert. He would be standing next to his horse's head, and when the camera had closed in to the point where the hero's head filled the whole screen, the hero would look the theater audience right in the eye while he addressed the very deliberate epithet to the absent villain. His lips would very slowly and obviously form the imprecation: *You . . . son . . . of . . . a . . . bitch!*

The effect was startling and comical; startling, because you could not believe, though you were seeing it, that the good guy was swearing. And it was comical because the good guy's expression while swearing was anything but vindictive. In fact, his expression indicated that he was struggling mightily to keep from bursting into laughter. His eyes twinkled; the corners of his lips kept twitching to restrain the smile fighting to get on his face. He looked as though he should have been silently labializing not the scripted execration but instead an amused, *You . . . bad . . . boy!*

My conjectures on why the good guy could not keep a straight face while delivering his malediction is that no matter how much he may have rehearsed his silent mouthing of the line and no matter how many retakes he occasioned, he could not survive the thought of the coming shock to the movie audience; or perhaps the line was not scripted and the director had him deliver it without rehearsal and did not bother with a retake; and maybe some jokester standing next to the camera silently mouthed an obscenity back at the actor to try to make the actor laugh. Anyway, as I said, the scene ended up on film as startling and comical.

On the other hand, the ending scene was almost always as expected: the standardized kiss bestowed upon the bashful cowboy by the ultra-nice girl. They would be standing and facing each other and in profile to the audience. He would be silent, or sometimes blurting "uhs" and "ers" while looking down, shuffling his feet, and crumpling the hell out of his Stetson. She would give him a soft smile and stare at him encouragingly with widened eyes, and when he failed to respond to these blandishments she would take matters into her own hands, literally. She would take his hands in hers and pull them around behind her, and then, with his arms thus encircling her, she would release his hands and put her arms around him, and she would snuggle against him. These actions would so raise the spirits of the good guy that he would lift the little girl up until they were face-to-face (the cowboy was always at least a foot taller than the girl), the camera would close in until only the two heads in full profile were on the screen, and the girl would initiate the nose-to-nose kiss on the lips.

This kiss was the signal for the little kids in Saturday matinee audiences to go berserk. During the long-held osculation and until "The End" flashed on the screen, they would shout, scream, stamp their feet, throw things, and slam their seats—all except me, it seemed. I would sit still through the bedlam and try calmly to contemplate the scene. It seems that I had a habit of reacting to events, on many occasions, differently than many of my peers.

(... What happened to sex? Well, the subject is intermingled with what I'm relating. Sex experiences didn't occur in a vacuum; in fact, they were usually incidental to other ongoing experiences. So that actually I'm giving you my growing sexual awareness in context with the passage of time. Never fear; sex is soon to predominate in my discourse, at the point where I enter fifth grade. For now, I'll finish the comment on the movie houses; then I'll reveal two poignant incidents that happened in my house, and then I'll proceed to sex. I was going to say platonic sex, but that expression is, if not oxymoronic, at least misleading and ambiguous. I mean if you want a woman's body [or head], that's sexual; if you don't get it, too bad, but you're still being sexual; platonic means you are not sexually interested in her body [or head]. So you shouldn't say platonic sex to mean sex without intercourse, if intercourse is desired. You might say platonic relationship, if that's what you mean, or unconsummated sexual relationship, if that's what you intend.)

You notice that Christ had it straight when He said in Saint Matthew 5:28, "But I say unto you, that whosoever looketh on a woman to lust after her hath committed adultery with her already in his heart," the heart being then considered the seat of the emotions. Were He addressing His audience today, He might have said, instead, " . . . hath committed adultery with her already with his hard-on." And this is the kind of adultery I committed at age ten, while in the fifth grade. But I'm getting ahead of myself, as I am still telling you how it was when I was in the third and fourth grades of school, in 1927 and 1928.

All movie houses showed at least a cartoon film, a

newsreel, and a feature film, usually in that order. The medium-class theaters added amateur nights, prize nights on which chinaware dishes were either given away or won, or both. And the deluxe movie houses, the movie palaces, provided vaudeville, which was a variety stage show, before the main feature or, if there happened to be a double feature showing, between the two main features.

The vaudevillians were excellent performers whatever their speciality, acrobats, dancers, singers, musicians, jugglers, magicians, comedians, even burlesque queens (modest ones). I particularly enjoyed a female monologist who came onstage with a donkey that she tethered near the wing by which she entered. She wore tights and had draped around her waist an American flag. At one point in her monologue she mentioned that many men had fought under that flag. At the end, she bent forward slightly toward the audience, rising to the balls of her feet and extending her arm toward the tethered donkey, which she had ignored during the whole of her monologue, and declared saucily, "If you didn't like my act," pointing her finger prettily at the donkey, "you can kiss my ass!"

I have even fonder memories of another female monologist, who spoke in Italian for the benefit of the Italian community, most of which consisted of families of immigrants who were only moderately familiar with English. She performed at a special show staged for the purpose, and I happened to be in attendance even though my knowledge of Italian was skimpy. She came to center stage in widow's weeds (black mourning garments), with her skirt just above the floor. There were no props. Solemnly she explained to the audience that her husband, a very strict man, had just died and that she had buried him in the backyard just outside the kitchen window here, and she pointed to her left.

Then she went to the imaginary window, raised it, and leaning out yelled to her dead husband, "Elmo! How is it out there? Are you comfortable? Since you're gone, I have become more active socially. Remember how you wouldn't let me dance, Elmo? Watch this," and she stepped back from the window and danced a little jig. "And remember you wouldn't let me lift my dress above the ankle? Well, what do you think of this?" Still facing the window, and in black silhouette to the audience, she slowly raised her skirt to midthigh and raised a very shapely leg toward her buried husband. "Do you see that, Elmo?" she teased, cocking her foot back and forth for emphasis. She went on in this vein for about twenty minutes while I laughed silently in appreciation of her witty taunting of the buried husband as she postured and grimaced before the window opening onto his grave. But even as I admired her performance I felt sympathy for her, because she was sophisticated and her audience was not, a tragic mismatch. It must have been a hard night for her, but she made it a wonderful one for me and I still applaud her when she comes on in my memory.

Of course, movies weren't the only mass entertainment, but they were constantly available. Less frequent live mass entertainment came in the forms of circuses, carnivals, medicine man shows, traveling evangelists, and traveling cultural (speaking) tours.

My most vivid memory of the circus recalls the debris left behind on the empty lot after the huge tents had folded and the circus had moved on to the next engagement city. The female performers had discarded many bloodstained folded cloths that we children referred to as cunt rags. A woman in her menses was said to have the rag on. Contrast this frank language with the delicate expression I later encountered in houses of prostitution: "She's having her flowers."

The carnivals left me with some permanent memories, each from sideshows in different midways. On the occasion of one show in particular, I became a bit dubious about scientists. It was nothing so traumatic as discovering that schoolteachers can be wrong, but a sort of disappointment at science's neglect of puzzling phenomena and a nagging suspicion that perhaps scientists were consciously avoiding difficult problems. (What the hell am I talking about? I'm talking about a—look; you didn't even let me get started. I . . . I am sticking to the subject. . . . All right, I'll describe the act first and comment on it afterwards. You aren't by any chance having your monthlies?)

When I entered the sideshow, I found myself in front of a strange stepladder. Instead of steps, there were three timber saws mounted in vertical slots, tooth side up. These were the single-handled one-man type of saw, about four feet long and five inches wide. They were mounted a foot apart, measuring the distance vertically between the toothed parts, so that the platform was three feet above and set back from the teeth of the lowest saw.

By the side of this apparatus stood a small, dark-skinned man who, for whatever reason, struck me as being from the Caribbean Sea area. He was barefoot, and he explained that he was going to ascend the ladder of saws in his bare feet and when he reached the platform he was going to jump down onto the teeth of the bottommost saw! And he did! This was one of those stupendous feats that you don't believe possible when it is proposed, while you're seeing it done, or when it has been accomplished. How can one stand barefoot on the toothed vertical edge of a saw without sinking down on it? How can one jump down three feet on it without its penetrating the soles of the feet, merely leaving only indentations in the flesh? And how can one jump down three feet onto a saw edge, even an untoothed saw edge, and land balanced so as not to fall, slip off, or break one's ankles?

It flashed upon me as I pondered these questions that the answers were not only unknown, but neither was there an effort being made to discover them. Where was the vaunted curiosity of science to explain these mystifying feats? Thus I came to my first realization that science tends to avoid allocating significant time and money to research of certain difficult but intriguing phenomena.

Take, for instance, some mysteries in the biophysical domain, besides this one of walking and jumping on saw edges. How to explain the cataleptic state induced by hypnotists in which the subject, stretched between the backs of two chairs, supports the weight of the hypnotists standing on his rigid body? What about all the other hypnotic effects? There are few attempts to explain walking on embers without harm to the walker or the apparent insensibility to pain when pins, knives, or other objects are thrust through the flesh of some people; there are other less consistent, strange results of severe impacts on the human body such as those from being struck by a speeding automobile or falling from a considerable height, with little or even no harm done to the victim.

Now I personally have experienced a strange biophysical phenomenon from time to time, one that I believe has been experienced by every male who shaves his face. At very infrequent and random intervals, while shaving, I will suddenly get the idea that there seems to be no razor blade in my razor. Yet another application of the razor results in hair being removed, but with absolutely none of the usual accompanying sensations of scratching sounds or pulls on the flesh, just a gliding of the razor so smoothly that it seems for certain there can be no blade in the razor. But an examination reveals that a blade is there. So easily is the hair removed that I have actually tested whether I could rub it off with my fingertips! How wonderful if one could shave like that every time! Scientists, what causes that hair condition? To hell with space exploration; get on this faceshaving problem.

Further, it seems to me that scientists tend to avoid the so-called psychic phenomena. I'm not speaking of the weird, conjectural, or unusual, but rather of the common and probably universally experienced kind that induce feelings or emotions in people, as in the case of instant like or love, instant dislike or hate, the feeling that eyes are upon you, the felt flash of mutual unspoken understanding or consent or dissent, or the mild electric-shock type of tingling sometimes experienced by one in the presence of another person.

Regarding the eyes-are-upon-you syndrome, I had a unique experience while standing in the empty lot between houses in the two adjacent lots. The feeling that someone somewhere behind me was observing me was so strong that I felt as though two eyeballs were pressing on my back. I bore it as long as I could before turning around to discover whether someone was staring at me. No one was in sight. I looked at the windows in the houses across the alley, but I saw no one in the windows. There was no feeling of eyes on me while I faced toward the alley, so after waiting a short while I faced about, and immediately I experienced the same sensation of eyes on my back. Again I turned toward the alley, saw no one, and felt no eyes on me. Just to double-check, I faced about again and felt the eyes on my back as palpably as though someone were pressing against me with the flat of his hand. I gave it up and just walked away from the empty lot. I can't begin to theorize about such a puzzling experience, and neither, I suspect, can the scientists.

Can it be that the hunch is related to the feeling of eyes upon you? Again you are confronted with a feeling of certainty or conviction about a situation, but with the difference that there is no ascribable possible cause for such a feeling. It simply grabs you. Say you are at the racetrack (let's assume it has the jockey-on-a-horse flat racing, which I prefer to harness racing) and you are languidly looking through the morning sheet, the schedule of races for the day. In the listing for the third race your eyes encounter horse number six: Deflowered. A strong feeling surrounds your entire body and encapsulates you. You become utterly convinced in all your being that the winner is—not will be, *is*—Deflowered in the third. It is as certain as the tides, sunrise, the seasons, death and taxes. Knowing better, laughing tolerantly at yourself and hoping you don't look as foolish as you feel, you make the bet at the two-dollar window—and you lose. It's a good thing you lose. A win could make you a compulsive hunch bettor and lead you inevitably to poverty and dereliction.

Still more interesting, psychically, is the feeling that you are experiencing a mild electric shock in the presence of some other person. Now this is not that feeling of bliss or attraction inspired in you on occasion by the presence of one of the opposite sex. I'll deal with that feeling in connection with sexual attraction, which I . . . (. . . Of course I'll discuss sex. I just . . . I know I promised. But I'm trying to keep to a reasonable time context as I go. Things happen contemporaneously as well as serially, and I am trying to give you the flavor of the times when the incidents of which I speak occur. . . . Your favorite flavor is brevity?

An interesting expression, that. I take your meaning. Just to relax you, I am now advising you that I will pursue sex (and other subjects) when I enter the fifth grade of school. At the moment in the third- and fourth-grade time frame.... How long before I get into fifth grade? Just let me say that I did not fail third or fourth grades.... That horrible groan! Your blanched face! Those tremors! Here; lie back, dear friend. That's it—loosen your belt; take deep breaths. Close your eyes. Now, let's see, where was I?)

Yes, about this feeling in someone's presence as though you were in contact with a "live" wire and experiencing that tingling sensation of an electric shock and there being no sense of attraction or repulsion on your part for the person who is the apparent cause of your reaction. You simply feel the tingling, which persists as long as the other person is present, and of course you become curious about the tingling and about the tingler. Usually (I say "usually" though this is an infrequent occurrence) you are rather close to the tingler, say within a room's width, but I experienced this phenomenon once at a distance of about thirty feet.

It was close to midnight as I happened to be standing in front of the railroad station that was in the heart of downtown. The building was old, with a plain wood floor, and had dim lighting for the large, high-ceilinged hall. There were two sets of entrance doors, the outer doors being latched, and about six feet beyond these there was a set of swinging doors. High up on the right wall as one entered was a large, round clock with Roman numerals for the hours. I decided to find out what time it was, and to that end I entered the station.

As I opened one of the inner doors, and while my hand was still pushing on it, I felt throughout my body a strong tingling sensation as though I were experiencing a mild electric shock. Apparently I was immersed in what physicists call a field of force, an electric or magnetic or electromagnetic or some other kind of field. I looked across the dim hall at the only other occupants, a group of three standing huddled together as they awaited their train. They were apparently a man and wife with their grown daughter. They had all been startled, and they jerked their heads toward me at the sound of my entrance.

To allay their possible fear of harm from me, I immediately turned my head toward the big clock on the wall and walked toward it, slowly sizzling all the while. In my brief glance at the trio I saw only blurs for their faces in the dimness of the place. They wore coats, for the season was cool. And though I assumed that the young woman was the radiating source of the tingling I felt, there was no reason for me to make that assumption other than that I preferred it. Since I could make out neither face nor form, I could rule out a visual (sexual) cause for the effect, leaving only the presence of the person as the cause. The moment I left the station, the tingling stopped. I wonder, during such encounters, does the other person feel a tingling, also? I doubt it.

But enough of the biophysical and psychic puzzles; let me turn to the realm of physics instead. I don't like to ask scientists about certain inexplicable but very apparent phenomena because it embarrasses them, which embarrasses me. On the other hand, I become somewhat peeved at their avoidance of some phenomena of physics. I'll be brief. (. . . You're welcome.) Transparency. How strange that some materials can be seen through, even through considerable thicknesses, while other materials are opaque even in very thin sections. Even more strange, to me, is the fact that some of the transparent materials, like glass and water, do not have an ordered atomic or molecular structure, which, intuitively, I would expect them to have, while some of the opaque materials, like sheets of lead or aluminum, do have an orderly array of atoms in their structure, which as far as transparency is concerned I would not intuitively expect them to have. It's easy to get the impression that nature has it backward, that you should be able to see through an orderly structure of atoms or molecules more easily than through a disarray. But of course nature can't be wrong about anything, though it can be seemingly perverse. I would like to know of even a half-assed theory to explain transparency. I myself have a quarter-assed theory, but I'm not going to tell anybody; let the savants mull the phenomenon over for themselves.

Now, color. What is it in the structure of a colored material that causes it to have that color when white light illuminates it? Suppose that you are looking at two objects, side by side and illuminated by the sun. Say one is blue and the other is red. What is in the makeup of the blue object that causes it to reflect the blue component of the sunlight while absorbing the other color components? Similarly for the red object; what makes it select red to reflect? Even I don't have a theory to explain this effect.

And then there are those marvelous forces at a distance: gravitational, magnetic, and electromagnetic. By what mechanism do they operate even through a vacuumed space to seize an object and move it or try to move it? How do they apply force on an object without actually laying hands on it, so to speak? Intuition says there must be some sort of laying on of "hands." To give the scientists their due, they have devoted tremendous effort to explain this phenomenon, but to date they remain empty-

"handed." (I'm sorry, I just couldn't resist making that remark.)

One final tidbit. The rising or setting sun (or moon) looks considerably bigger, say half again as big in diameter, as when it is high in the sky, doesn't it? Refraction and dispersion of the sun's rays by the atmosphere may contribute a little something to this effect, but it's mainly something else that does it, as I can demonstrate:

On a three-by-five-inch piece of plain white paper, print in block letters three-eighths of an inch high a word, say *BOOK*. Hold this at arm's length in front of you; then quickly raise it above your head. The letters appear smaller! Apparently the flexible structures of the eye vary with position and change its magnifying power.

Thus I have concluded my discourse on puzzling phenomena.... (A long-lived sigh, that. A vast sigh, of which the unburdening of yourself must surely ease your disposition, which I have noted tends to the choleric betimes. ... I will not shut up. I have just as much a right to talk as you have.... I told you—sex comes later. Right now I have a headache. Allow me to resume my discourse on mass entertainments.)

I attended a revival meeting once, in a huge tent pitched on a large open space in the heart of the city. The evangelist was nationally famous. My older sister, a performer's sweetheart type of person—she enjoyed all forms of entertainment somewhat uncritically and rarely expressed displeasure with any of it—just had to take in this tent revival and, I don't know how it came about, took me along. For my part, I intended to be very critical. (I was a passionate child critic on things religious.) We paid to enter the great tent and found that it was filled with wooden benches. The entire ground area had been covered with wood shavings, not to keep dust from rising, for the surface was grassy, but to provide a cover against the moisture left by the previous day's rain. An usher led us in a spongy walk to our places. The great evangelist spoke from a rostrum on the high wooden dais, and he skillfully interspersed his sonorous religious drivel with witty and humorous commentary and asides. After ten minutes had elapsed, I rated him excellent for elocution, fine for entertaining interludes, and rotten for subject matter. One such show, that one, was to last me a lifetime.

But my older sister did much better for me on another occasion. Again she took me to a grassy open area on one end of which a tent was pitched. However, this open area was a corner lot, and the tent was a small pyramidal one, perhaps ten feet by ten feet, with a flap extension serving as a shield from the sun. In front of the tent was a small wooden platform about four feet wide by three feet deep, raised about four feet above the ground. It was designed to accommodate two people, who mounted it by means of a set of steps at the rear of the platform.

By now you have probably guessed, correctly, that my sister took me to a medicine show. We went for the entertainment, but my sister had an ulterior motive, also, which was revealed after the first show. Now this was a sort of latter-day medicine show; rather, it was one of the last of a passé art form, small open-air theater to attract prospective purchasers of a product offered for sale. As the impresario mounted the small flight of stairs to the platform, he illustrated the end of an era through the clothing he wore. Instead of buckskins, there was apparel of fine cloth: long pants with wide cuffs and a loose tailored jacket. The only concession to the not-so-old West was a large Stetson on his head. Or was it a concession? I believe the Stetson was worn not to give an impression, primarily—it's a heavy weight to have on the head during a hot sunny day—but to act as a temporary sun shade. It was revealed in the course of his pitch to the thirty or forty city hicks assembled for the free show that his cure-all nostrum was not the classical snake oil but instead was a magical concoction that contained, I believe he said, something to do with fish. Yes, I'm sure that there was something fishy about it.

Toward the end of his spiel, an assistant brought up to the platform a case of the elixir and shills unobtrusively infiltrated the crowd. Then the peddler turned over the proceedings to his seller assistant and descended the platform to be replaced by a second seller. The hawking began, with buying brisk at first. As buying wavered, the shills became active to encourage the reluctant, and finally, as buying almost stopped, one of the sellers would announce that a few more bottles of the cloudy liquid needed to be sold before the show could go on. Begrudgingly the few more bottles were bought, not by suckers, but by people who, in effect, were paying to put the show on. And I thank them.

The platform was cleared for the show, and the two vendors became two actors, two consummate actors. Their repertory consisted of skits, which were introduced by one or the other of the two with an explanation of the situation to be played out, and the introduction blended smoothly into the monologist's opening lines. At the proper time the other actor ascended to the minuscule stage where the two barely had room to move, and they captivated their audience.

In one marvelous skit, the scene was laid in a funeral parlor where, the first actor explained, he was upstairs, late at night, alone, and there was a corpse downstairs awaiting processing. Mind you, this show was going on outdoors at about three o'clock in the afternoon of a hot, sunny, and humid day. Yet the monologist was so effective that when a white-shrouded figure very slowly came up the steps to the platform and took up a position behind the oblivious speaker, chill tremors shook the beads of perspiration on the backs of the viewers. This ghost was a black man, as was evident from his face, which was visible under the white hood of the shroud, and when from time to time he slowly swayed from the waist and showed his hooded head over the speaker's shoulder, gasps, screams, and shouts rent the air of the bright day. Such was the skill of these itinerant players.

There was a lull after the show as the audience dispersed, during which my sister led me around to the tent flap under which the impresario was seated on a folding chair before a folding table. He was not wearing his Stetson. After my sister and I were provided with folding chairs, she explained to him that I suffered from asthmatic attacks and asked him whether his medicine would help me, much to my embarrassment at her simplicity. He had listened languidly as he perspired, and when my sister asked her question he languidly replied that the medicine would be good for me. My sister bought a bottle of it. I honestly cannot recall what became of that bottle, but I know this: I drank none of it.

6
Physicians, Buttocks, and Genitalia in Language

Now, as I am a man of my word . . . (. . . I am a worthy man? . . . I am a wordy man. Your diction is lousy. Are you saying I am a worthy man or a wordy man? . . . I am a wordy worthy man, or is it a worthy wordy man? Are you paying me an ambidextrous compliment? Never mind. You will recall that I mentioned I would apprise you of two incidents that occurred in my house. They have to do with an old profession, . . . Not that old profession, you dumb . . . in my house? You know, you must be one of those guys of whom it is said that if you split his skull open, vulvae would spill out. The incidents have to do with the practice of medicine, a practice that, in my opinion, has a long way to go to become proficient. In fact, I do not seek a physician's advice when I am very sick; I have my health to think about. So that when I'm too sick to see a doctor, I wait till I have improved somewhat. This tactic preserves some leeway in case he worsens my condition. My parents were very wise in this regard, consulting a physician only when they felt they were in extremis, or at least not too far removed from it. And I used to think them so old-fashioned and unreasonable for it. Well, let me continue.)

The physician's preferences, hence the candidates for

children's diseases of my day, were tonsillitis and adenoiditis, and preferably both together. This twin plague was firmly settled in the land, and most children's symptoms seemed to indicate tonsilloadenoidectomy. My next younger brother fell victim to this procedure, which was carried out in the front room of my house. Anyone was free to watch as my brother was stretched out on a table, a white sheet placed over his body, and a gauze mask placed over his face. The physician instructed my brother to count slowly to ten as ether was dripped slowly onto the gauze. My brother's counting stopped before reaching ten, and the physician went to work. An interesting aftermath to this operation occurred over a decade later, when this same physician was examining this same brother and the physician remarked that a terrible job had been done in extracting my brother' tonsils and adenoids and asked to know who was the butcher who had performed the operation.

My turn was yet to come, some five years later, but in a hospital, as the operations for these fashionable diseases persisted for a couple decades, gradually subsiding to be replaced eventually by the hysteria for hysterectomy, a concession to women, which in turn became superseded by the mania for coronary heart bypasses, to give men their turn on the chopping block.

This penchant for cutting people up, you realize, is nothing new. The hands-down all-time winner for unnecessary operations is, of course, circumcision, which has been going on since about 1900 B.C., if you take for your authority the Bible, King James Version, Genesis 17:10, when God told Abraham to start chopping.

Another physician made a call at my house one night after I had gone to bed. I was awakened by screams and moans from my mother in the next room. I was not allowed to get out of bed and could only shiver as my mother's agonized cries continued at irregular intervals for hours, and I fell asleep not knowing what her trouble was. When I was up and about in the morning I wandered into the middle room of the house and found there, on the treadle sewing machine, which had its wooden cover down, a beautiful baby girl all decked out in a fluffy dress and wearing a cap and booties, as though ready for a buggy ride.

I walked to her side and stared at the gorgeous little girl, who strongly resembled my mother. She didn't seem to be breathing, but she looked so healthy that I felt she had to start breathing soon. I waited for what seemed a long time to see a rising and falling of the little chest, but there was no motion. Finally, I turned away.

And now for sex. (. . . What the . . . Stop cheering. . . . Stop it, I say. O thou bright-eyed! Thou agitated! Hast no concern for decorum? Cease thy bellowing, which serves only to encork [a nonce word] thine ear. Prithy, muffle thine ardor, thus uncorking thine ear which lend me the while I discourse. Attend me closely, o salacious, and your lechery will gain reward. So list or, if you prefer, hearken.)

Since most of the big guys were unemployed during the depression, they were often gathered in groups and engaged in discussion, whether in the alley, in front of the grocery store, or around someone's car parked at the curb. And occasionally some of the kids would find themselves at the fringe of a group and listen for a while to the chatter. At times when I listened the talk was about girls, and the expression, "piece of ass" was often used, to my puzzlement, because it was obvious from the context that anal intercourse was not being discussed. The use of the expression never failed to annoy me because it was so inapt. Why didn't they say a "a piece of pussy"? Why this predilection for *ass?* Let me pursue this subject.

To begin with a simple case first, consider the use of *ass* (a part) to designate "a woman, or women, considered as sexual partner(s)" (the whole person or persons). This figure of speech where a part designates the whole thing, or vice versa, is called synecdoche. For example, in this case, "Is she *ass?*" means "is she a *woman* who engages in sexual intercourse?," which colloquially is usually interpreted as, "Does she fuck?" Or again, "I went to this party, see, and there was a lot of *ass* there," means that there were *women* at the party who were, or were reputed to be, or were hoped to be promiscuous.

Using these examples for comparison, it becomes evident that the expression "a piece of ass" is a more complex figure of speech than a simple synecdoche. For here, unless specifically indicated otherwise by the utterer, the expression refers to vaginal, not anal, (and not oral) intercourse with a woman. *Ass* in this expression is used to represent its opposite, "pussy" (a part of speech called antiphrasis) and used again to represent the whole woman (synecdoche).

There is another common use of antiphrasis (the accent is on the second syllable) in a context that is usually not sexual, though sexual terms are used. A brief discussion of the slang term involved is in order here. The first term is *prick,* used to designate penis. My guess for this usage is that the penis, by metonymy (calling something by the name of something else), is called a *prick,* a pointed object that can penetrate, in rough comparison to the erect penis, which can penetrate. Another name for penis, this time by a double metonymy, is cock. The male of the chicken, a rooster, is called a cock; by comparison of mannerism, a swaggering *man* was probably called a *cock* because of his cocky mannerism (first metonymy); then an erect *penis,* thought of as a jaunty little man, was called a *cock* by comparison with its cocky owner (second metonymy).

And yet another term for this discussion is *cunt,* the impolite for vulva. In Latin, it's *cunnus;* in Elizabethan English, it's *queynte. Cunt* and *pussy* are used interchangeably, but not so in the antiphrasis that we can now examine, nor in the expression for fellator, or fellatrix, which is always "cocksucker," never "pricksucker."

Very often, a man who feels that he has been badly used by another man will call the perceived offender a prick, never a cock in such case, but a prick, probably because he felt "I've been fucked!" (Taken advantage of, remember?) This sort of offensive name calling is termed *aeschrologia* and is combined with our antiphrasis in the expression "he's a cunt!" In this sense, the utterer means that the offender is an unmitigated prick, a royal prick, a superprick, so that *cunt* serves as an intensifier to indicate the extent of outrage felt by the fuckee. "He's a cunt!" is always declaimed explosively and with flashing eye, and though expecting it, I have never heard it said with a stamp of the foot in accompaniment.

This particular antiphrasis occurs in Italian, too, and probably in every other language. But in Italian it occurs with a peculiar reversal. One way of saying "Fuck you!" in Italian is 'Sto cazzo. [*questo cazzo*—this prick—"in your ass" is understood]!" But often as not this is changed to " 'sta minghia" or " 'sta minchia [*questa minchia*—this cunt—again "in your ass" is understood]," which expression could be very confusing to a bystander not conversant with such street language or with a discussion such as this.

Such a bystander would probably be as confused as I

was when I encountered the expression "a piece of ass." (. . . That's right—I did say that I would pursue *ass,* not *prick* or *pussy,* as a matter for discourse, but it's so easy for one thing to lead to another. I will probe the apparent obsession for the word *ass* in the USA—it's *arse* in other English-speaking countries—but first a caveat: remember the exceptions to the interchangeability of *prick* with *cock* and *pussy* with *cunt. Never* say, "He's a cock," or, "He's a pussy," or, "[S]He's a pricksucker," you will in such case probably puzzle your hearer; your poor usage will cause embarrassment at your lack of command of the language and cause him to wonder about your educationally handicapped background and your retarded overcoming of it. . . . You promise to watch your language? Good. Now let me acquaint you a little more with my milieu at the time of my early grade school years, in the early 1920s. . . . You were afraid of this. Well . . .)

7

The Times, "Ass" in Speech, Workaday World

The earliest newspaper headlines I can recall had to do with scandals involving the president (Harding). Also in the news was the case before the Supreme Court involving the question of the constitutionality of the Nineteenth Amendment, concerning women's suffrage. An adult relative of mine opined to me that women "should not have the vote"; I silently disagreed. (This same person stated to me on another occasion that colleges were no good because they taught that there is no God; I silently agreed with the colleges.) Newspapers were sold for two cents per copy, but extra editions hawked by boys circulating through neighborhood streets and yelling, "Extra!" sold for three cents. It did not need a major happening to serve as an excuse for an extra edition; something like the fatal shooting of a local minister at his pulpit, for example, was a sufficient trigger.

As for radios, few people had them, so that, to listen to the broadcast of a world heavyweight boxing match, for instance, people assembled in front of the newspaper building where a loudspeaker attached to a radio was installed at the second-story level.

Delivery of mail by airplane was still a hazardous undertaking, as evidenced by news of frequent crashes due mainly to the lack of good information on aviation weather.

The movement for birth control was in the making, but information and advice on birth control and abortion were still taboo. I recall seeing a group of people standing in front of a house down the street where a friend of mine lived. When I joined the group and asked why they were there, I was told that a physician had been sent for because my friend's older sister had used lye to induce an abortion and was seriously ill. Fortunately, she recovered.

But let me return to the subject of the prominence of "ass" in speech. If a woman in a short dress be taken in profile, one notes three prominences: tit, ass, and leg, rather calf of the leg. According to his preference for a particular prominence, one classifies himself as a tit man, an ass man, or a leg man. In my case, I can't make up my mind. In confrontation, I think I'm a tit man; next thing I know a certain curvature of ass makes me an ass man; then I might find myself walking behind a curvy pair of legs and feel a stirring between my thighs that tells me I must be a leg man. This inability to classify myself had me so worried that I once contemplated consulting a psychiatrist about it, but I wisely forebore. Instead I meditated on the problem and sought to discover what it is about certain curved surfaces that excites one sexually.

What specific shape of the mamma (breast) makes me a tit man? What particular shapes of the glutei (the three muscles forming each buttock) make me an ass man? What singular shape of gastrocnemius muscle (calf of the leg) makes me a leg man? I have a confession to make. At times I believe that I am a mouth man because certain shapes of orbicularis oris (the round muscle of the mouth) result in lips that excite me from my head down to my—well, they make me feel as though part of me is trying to get up. Most of the time these appurtenances on a female are merely interesting to the male observer, but occasionally their curves are such that the sight of them causes some degree of sexual arousal. Who knows how and why this happens? I'll not ponder the problem further, and I don't believe that scientists will ponder it at all. It's just another tough one for them to avoid.

Unless a person is wearing tentlike clothing, a body protuberance is usually apparent, the most prominent one being, usually, the ass. I'm speaking of people who are not unusually shaped, as are very big-titted women or men and women who apparently have no ass to speak of. These latter straight-up-and-down types are said to be flat as a pine board, and some of these tend to have huge bellies. But, taken all in all, what stands out in a man or woman seen at any distance is the ass. So that it would seem only natural when making disrespectful reference to anyone to couple the remark with that most prominent feature.

Here we have:
Ass, piece of ass— already discussed
Chippie—a little piece (of ass); has fallen into disuse
Smartass—wiseguy
Move your ass—hurry up
Get the lead out of your ass, or shortened to get the lead out—hurry up
Your ass is mud—you're doomed
Your footlocker is your own, but your ass belongs to the commanding officer (military)— you have little choice but to comply; your personal freedom is limited
Up your ass—fuck you; go to hell

Fuck you in the ass—go to hell
Va fa entro culo (Italian)—literally, go do it in the ass; fuck you

Let's get more specific and talk about a subunit of the ass, the asshole. Of yore, the postal abbreviation for the state of Ohio was O., for example Dayton, O. This led some wags who found themselves behind a dog with a stub tail, which left its asshole exposed, to exclaim, "Oh, look, there's a dog from Ohio!" The observer of such a sight was almost inevitably induced to remark on it because the view of an asshole is an uncommon sight, unless the observer happens to be a proctologist, and it is a compelling sight, almost hypnotic. The memory of it is vivid and lasting. And if it should so happen that shortly after his viewing the observer is subjected to some sudden stress, say a boor steps on his toe, it's easy to believe that the observer might spontaneously associate this disturbing experience with the one caused by the dog and blurt out, "You asshole!" Once having made this association, such an observer would thenceforth tend to apply the appellation, verbally or mentally, to any male person who happened to exasperate him. Only males are thought of by men as "assholes." Women, in similar circumstances, are thought of by men as pains in the ass.

Now I have been examining this subject from the viewpoint of a city dweller. A rural inhabitant, in a farm environment, would very likely have come to use the same expression inspired by a pig's anus. There is another expression inspired by the pig's anus, "in the pig's asshole," which means, curiously, "absolutely not." The short form, "in the pig's ass," is more often used. Examples are:

Go with you? In the pig's asshole.
In the pig's ass you will!
Hey, Joe, loan me a dollar. Reply: Pig's ass.
And the last verse of a soldier's drinking song goes:

Glorious! Glorious! One keg of beer for the four of us.
We'll hoist Old Glory to the top of the pole
And we'll all reenlist—in the pig's asshole!

It should be mentioned here that those who use the expression "in the pig's asshole" also employ the epithet *pigfucker,* which is to say "dirty bastard," or the like. Probably the early usage was meant literally. Time has taken its usual toll, so that the expression is little in vogue now, having been replaced by "motherfucker," which I believe came from the hillbillies in whose environment incest was common, and who defined a virgin as a twelve-year-old girl who could outrun her older brother.

Before I tell you more of what I overheard from the big boys when they gathered on the street, let me apprise you of the workaday world of the time as I saw it.... (No, I am not putting the subject of ass behind me. There is more to come, and it ties in with homosexuality, which is something else I heard discussed by the big guys. Patience, friend.)

All the grocery stores, even the chain stores, were small, and in order to supply the large number of industrial workers in town, there were very many such stores. In my block alone, there were five! Two were on one corner, one near the other corner, and two were in midblock and only two doors from each other. And since home iceboxes were small, food that needed cooling was purchased as closely as possible to the intended time for consumption, to alleviate the need for storage space. To this end, and to accommodate the shiftworkers who bought their lunch foods just before leaving for work, the grocery stores opened at five o'clock in the morning and closed at midnight. They also provided another service for their customers. When one had an emergency, he ran to the grocery store to use its telephone.

On occasion my mother would send me to our grocery store, the nearest one, just two doors away, to buy two or three items that I tried to keep in mind by repeating them to myself over and over, usually with lip-movement accompaniment. If a couple of lady customers happened to be ahead of me in the store, as at times it so happened, they would usually be engaged in conversation with the woman grocer about the local priest (an Irishman, of course), who, it seemed from their conversation, never ceased asking for more money from his parishioners. When the grocer would notice my lips silently forming my intended order, she would excuse herself to wait on me.

I mention this because it leads to the story of a little girl similarly situated who had arrived while this same grocer was relating to her two women customers the story of an accident that had happened to a woman friend of the three. The grocer broke off her telling to ask the little girl what she wanted before she might forget it. The little girl said, "A pound of peas," at which the grocer turned back to the two women customers and resumed her story, but at the point where she recited the victim's sustaining of the accident she broke off again to ask the little girl, "Split or whole?" and the little girl said, "Her did?" (Don't sneer. It's true.)

Well, I was probably buying some salami for my father's sandwiches for him to take to work. Salami was then a delicious and expensive luncheon meat of pork and beef, pepper, garlic, wine, and salt. Usually less expensive luncheon meats were bought, but the least expensive was least bought—not because it wasn't wholesome and tasty, but because it was not in style! We children dreaded being sent to the store for bologna because any customers present would snicker at us and even the storekeeper could barely keep from turning her lips down or rolling her eyes. So we children would look into the store before entering to make certain that there were not customers inside, and if there were, we would delay entering for as long as we dared for them to be waited on and depart. This irrational contempt for bologna was to persist for many more years before succumbing to the exigencies of the Great Depression.

Anyway, when my father departed for work with salami sandwiches, he would return from his twelve-hour shift at the aluminum mill with half of a sandwich in his jacket pocket and one of the children would reach in for the prize. But one day my father returned from work with a whole sandwich. He had witnessed a fellow worker's fall into the rollers that were fed sheets of aluminum and had seen the pulp that had been the worker scooped up with a shovel at the end of the line. It was to be three days before my father could resume his normal eating. I was not aware of any public notice taken of this industrial accident.

Although no accident was involved, I myself witnessed a work situation that still triggers little shivers when I see it in my imagination. The brick crossroad forming the east boundary of my block was being torn up preparatory to resurfacing it with asphalt, and work was in progress as I arrived at the junction of the alley with the crossroad. Two workmen were removing the surface there brick by brick. One of the workers squatted and with both hands held a large chisel upright between two bricks. He wore no goggles. The other worker swung a long-handled sledgehammer over his head and with great force brought it down on the chisel. As the sledgehammer started downward, the chisel holder would close his eyes, unable to bear the sight, I thought at the time, but now I realize that he was also shielding his eyes from possible flying sparks as metal crashed on metal. I was amazed at how steadily and upright he held the chisel, even while his eyes were closed; and I was equally amazed at the ability of the sledge wielder to end his mighty swing with a flat contact of the sledge onto the head of the chisel. I forced myself to watch several swings of the sledgehammer, and I trembled at the thought of the consequences of a less than perfect contact of sledge with chisel. I visualized the chisel holder as losing both hands at the wrists or having the chisel deflected into his body, or the chisel might be deflected into the legs of the sledge swinger.

Just then the foreman came by and I wanted to suggest to him that the chisel should be held by means of some sort of tongs, but one look at him convinced me that the safety of his workers was the last thing on his mind. I reflected that if either worker complained, he would be invited to quit, and that if the foreman mentioned worker safety to his superior, the foreman would be judged insane and summarily discharged. I silently hastened away.

For a less grim aspect of work conditions, I can recite about the walk homeward of workers employed at the coal yard that was about five blocks from my house. At a little after five o'clock in the afternoon, a group of five or six of them would pass my house. They would be walking on the sidewalk on the opposite side of the street, and their pace was very fast, apparently in anticipation of a hot supper awaiting them. They chattered gaily as they passed, but they also betrayed embarrassment because of their spectacular appearance. You see, they were all jet black with coal dust, face, hands, clothes, and all. The eyes and teeth of these animated coal piles gleamed against the dark backgrounds of their owners as the workers laughed and joked their way home. I wonder whether facilities for washing up and changing clothes were ever made available to these workers before the coal yard went out of business.

There was rigorous work going on inside the homes, too, as I appreciated when my mother asked me to spell her off in punching dough for bread or in turning the crank of the clothes wringer clamped to the washtub after the clothes had been scrubbed by hand on the scrubbing board and then rinsed. Handling the water for the wash process was heavy and somewhat hazardous work, the first step being to pour water by the bucket into a copper boiler. This vessel was twenty inches high, twenty inches long, and about a foot wide. The sides were parallel, but the ends were rounded and furnished with wood-covered handles so that by means of them the filled boiler could be lifted by two people onto the front part of the coal stove, so that it covered two of the four stove lids and the space between them that was directly over the fire.

After the water came to a boil, the boiler was lifted off the stove, carried down to the basement, and emptied into the washtub. Then the water temperature was adjusted by adding cold water, the soiled clothes were dumped in, soap chips were added, and after some soaking and agitation of the clothes by hand the scrubbing board was inserted to rest on the bottom and be supported by the rim of the washtub. The clothes were then scrubbed by rubbing them over the corrugated metal surface of the scrubbing board, after which the tub was emptied and another boiler full of hot water was poured in for the rinse. And after the rinse, as I mentioned before, the handwringer was clamped to the rim of the tub and the clothes were wrung through and then taken out in bushels to be hung on the clotheslines. It was work, work, work and more to come when the dried clothes were brought in, sprinkled with water, and balled up and set aside for a while so that the clothes would be uniformly humidified and not scorch when the heavy hand iron was heated and applied to them.

Often the coal stove's top and oven were fully in use, yet more cooking space was needed, so the two-burner kerosene stove on the opposite side of the kitchen was put to use. But even though the coal stove was not being fully utilized, the kerosene stove with its smoky wicks and glass chimneys would be used for quick heating of light meals. My mother tried to teach my younger sister how to cook using the kerosene stove, and one day in particular I empathized with my sister, who was absolutely disinterested and kept looking out the door of the kitchen into the beautiful day where her playmates were. Each time my sister attempted to edge toward the door, my mother would grab her arm and pull her back without interrupting her instruction on the cooking heat, the appearance of the frying food, the time necessary to cook, the spices to add. I felt so sorry for my sister—and for my mother, who was also missing a beautiful day outdoors.

But even though she seemed perpetually busy with other things, my mother found time to crochet, usually sitting by the sewing machine in the middle room and with her back to the window. The poor light didn't seem to bother her, and she did not wear glasses while she applied herself for hours at a time. I had no idea how much she produced in those days but was stunned later by the sight of some of her larger pieces, lengths of crocheting three feet wide and thirty feet long!— several of them.

Now ours was not one of those houses where the front room was a sacrosanct dining room. Such houses, as a rule, belonged to families with no more than four children, the practical reason being that larger families needed all the space available for active family use. A family of four children, in my neighborhood, was a small one; six to eight children was the norm; my mother had thirteen, counting stillborns and miscarriages. When visiting the house of a friend from a small family, I might be allowed to look into the front room, from the doorway, because no one, not even family members, entered there unless accompanied by the mother of the household. Such "dining" rooms were museum pieces. The floor, the dining table and chairs, the china cabinet all sparkled in their high gloss. Dust was not allowed. Use was not allowed. It was all for show, for fashion.

The china cabinet, about five feet high and about three feet wide, had a bowed glass front that allowed practically unobstructed visibility of the treasured chinaware. And once I had the privilege of being escorted to the china cabinet by a proud mother for a close look at the contents, never used, and never to be used.

In time, fashion demanded that a home should have a player piano, and to make room for it, the fiction of the "dining room" was discarded. Out went the dining room table and chairs, the china cabinet stayed, and in came the player piano, so that now the front room came to be used occasionally. Our player went into the middle room, where I soon learned that playing it was work. After the piano roll was inserted, two broad footpedals were depressed alternately to rotate the roll, whose paper was perforated with a pattern of small rectangular holes, and to actuate the pneumatic mechanism that squeezed air through the holes in the paper to depress the piano keys. We had rolls of the current popular songs and of some Italian songs. Particularly appealing to me was one named "La Morte Di Cesare [The death of Caesar]." I do not recall our having rolls of the folk songs which were to saturate the radio broadcasts, songs like "You Can't Kill an Old Horsefly" or "The Farmer Took Another Load Away."

8
Fear of the Dark

I'll have done with the inside of the house by recounting a great personal victory: the conquest of my irrational fear of the dark. The battle began one evening in the dark bedroom adjacent to the middle room. Usually the door at the left end of the bedroom was ajar. I did not feel comfortable on chancing to look at that deep black space between the jamb and the door, and when, on occasion, it was necessary to fetch something from the bedroom I would first open the door all the way before entering to let in as much light as possible and then I would go in and locate the pullchain on the ceiling lamp.

Common sense told me that I should not be afraid to enter the dark bedroom. So, as a start toward overcoming the fear, I forced myself to go into the dark bedroom without opening the door any wider than necessary to enter, therein to remain for a while with pounding heart, looking toward the light from the doorway and listening for the voices of whichever family members were in the house at the time. After a few repetitions, it came easily to enter the darkened bedroom and even stand with my back to the light from the partially open door while looking about into the dimness.

Before long after that, my courage was summoned to a greater test. I found myself alone in the house one evening. The lights were on in the kitchen, in the front room, and the middle room, where I stood looking at the blackness between the partially open bedroom door and the doorjamb. It was test time. As I felt anxiety rising within me, I decided to act quickly, before I might lose heart, so I stepped to the door and walked around it into the dim of the room. Then, with my back to the door, I reached back and closed it, an act that introduced me to a wondrous experience.

For a second or so I stared at what seemed solid blackness, but that changed to something quite different, a fine pattern of dim, dirty white points on a dark, but not deep-black, background. The sight can be likened to the appearance of a celestial naked-eye nebula seen on a moonless night. (. . . Please, don't groan like that. I'll give you a different simile, a more earthy one, to which you may relate more easily. Let's see. . . . Ah, how's this? I seemed to be standing at the center of a six-foot sphere whose surface was a dimly seen, extremely fine lacework. . . . That was all in my head? You're exactly right, it was, and here's how I proved it to myself—and you can verify it for yourself.) In a way it was annoying to have this tenuous veil hanging before my eyes; I thought to explain it. Finally I covered my eyes firmly with the palms of my hands. My view was unchanged. I quickly removed my hands from my eyes. No change. Apparently, in a dark room one sees matter in, on, and of the eye. There are occasional transient points of bright light, scintillations.

Since the shade on the window was slightly translucent and did not tightly fill the window frame, sufficient outside light filtered into the room to allow, after a few minutes of eye adjustment, the discernment of areas of a range of shades. Because of natural and usually brief retentivity of the image seen by the eye, if one stares at an isolated and relatively bright object or surface and then looks away, the image is still seen by the observer, so that the object appears to move or stop with the observer's eye motions, and in a darkened room, after a few minutes, the apparent motions of retained dim images result in an impression on the observer of swirling motions in the room if the eyes are being moved smoothly.

But if the observer, having lingered with his gaze on a relatively bright object or surface, suddenly shifts his gaze to a new direction, then the image appears to have jumped to the new direction, and this experience can chill the observer's scalp. It's hard to guard against because one tends to forget to say to himself, "Now, I'm going to turn my head; be ready for the image jump." Looking about in the dark takes some getting used to; it's almost always accompanied with some uneasiness, and there are thrills to be had. I did not realize it at the time, but in that dark bedroom I passed my crucial test in overcoming unreasoning fear of the dark. What I thought were more rigorous tests to come were denouement, anticlimax.

Of course, the next step in my antifear campaign was to enter all three dark bedrooms when there was no one in the house but myself. That was easy, so then I turned off all the lights in the house, in which the shades had already been drawn, and leisurely felt my way through all the rooms of the house in pitch-blackness, with no particular qualms; in fact, I enjoyed the reconnaissance. There remained . . . the basement.

And therein lie two or three tales, one involving sheer terror, with which I shall begin. The tale of sheer terror. When my mother would say to me, "Go down the cellar and get a bucket of coal for the stove," I would feel a narrow line of chill down the middle of my back, extending from the nape of my neck to the crease of my buttocks.

Now that I think of it, this might be the origin of the expression "you've got a yellow streak up [or down] your back," meaning you are afraid or cowardly, varied as in, "You're yellow-bellied," or simply, "You're yellow." Why yellow? Among other things, yellow has been used to symbolize cowardice, but not, to my knowledge, fear alone. As I have heard it often used, "Yellow!" was a taunt to incite to action a hesitator who might or might not be fearful. In the expression "yellow streak," the word "yellow" is symbolic, but the "streak" refers to an actual physiological experience, a chill and crawly feeling along a thin line, say two inches wide, extending the length of the vertical midline of the back.

Regardless of fear, there was no evading the task of filling the coal bucket, since all the children who were able took their turn at it. So, from behind the kitchen stove I would retrieve the near- empty coal bucket. It was made of black sheet metal and resembled an oblong garden sprinkling can in that it had a hoop handle for lifting and carrying, a handle at the back for tipping, and a wide spout for pouring. To stoke the stove, a lid lifter, which looked like a screwdriver with its tip bent at an angle, was inserted into a recess near the rim of the round stove lid, and the stove lid was then lifted off. A poker about eighteen inches long was inserted into the caked bed of coals and agitated to make holes for the free flow of air; then the coal-containing bucket would be lifted and tilted to pour in new coal to the fire. All this would be repeated when the other lid of the front of the stove was removed. After several hours, the grates on which the coals rested would be agitated by means of a hand crank to shake out the bottom layer of ashes from the burned coal. This was done briefly so as not to shake out live coals or even unfired coals. Then, by means of a small cast-iron flat shovel that resembled a rather large child's play shovel, the ashes shaken down were scooped out and transferred to an ash bucket.

When the ash bucket was full, it was taken to the basement and emptied into an ashcan, really an aluminum garbage can, which also received ashes from the coal furnace. And when the ashcan was full, or nearly so, it was carried out of the cellar by two people, by means of the two handles, and it was set down in the snow, often, in the middle of the backyard. An empty ashcan was placed nearby. Then ashes were tipped from the filled ashcan into a long-handled sifter, which was about four inches deep and slightly smaller than the ashcan in diameter. Now the filled sifter was lifted above the empty ashcan and shaken back and forth to break up the packed ash so that it could fall through with the loose ash and leave behind those unburned coals which inevitably escaped when the stove grates were agitated. Sifting ashes was another unloved job.

(... What does carrying out the ashes have to do with sex? Why, it's the inspiration for the phrase, "going out to get one's ashes hauled," meaning "going gashing or looking for a piece of ass." Often the cockhound (satyr) would preface such an announcement with a stamping of his feet and a nodding of his head while stating, "I'm hot to trot!" Then he would vow, "I'm going out to get my ashes hauled." ... You're sorry you asked. All right, you're forgiven. Now, let's see; I picked up the near-empty coal bucket ...)

The door to the basement was at the back corner of the kitchen, opposite the window through which my father had hurled a food can during his religious tantrum, remember? I flipped the light switch that turned on the cellar lights, opened the door to the staircase along the cellar wall, and descended into the first, and smaller, cellar. At the foot of the staircase was our one sanitary fixture, the toilet. (We had no bathtub then, and showers were rare in houses; we took sponge baths in tubs.) A half-turn to the left brought me to one of two openings into the second cellar, "the big cellar," in the center of which stood the coal-fired furnace, around which I walked to reach the coal pile under the cellar window.

Before filling the coal bucket, I checked the furnace fire by pushing back the slide on the furnace door and peering in through the round holes thus uncovered. If much ash was evident among the glowing coals, the furnace needed stoking, so the first thing to be done was to agitate the grates by means of a heavy crank. Often large clinkers that had formed would not go through the grates, so I would open the furnace door, and by means of a poker, a half-inch-thick steel rod about six feet long with a handle at one end and a right-angle bend at the other end, I would break the clinkers. Sometimes the clinkers wouldn't break, necessitating using the hook of the poker to pull them out through the furnace door and onto the cellar floor.

After transferring the ash and clinkers to the ashcan, I shoveled coal into the furnace and spread it smoothly over the glowing coals. Then, with the furnace door closed, I walked around the furnace to the chimney duct, which connected the furnace and the chimney. There I adjusted, if necessary, the two air-flow controls in the duct, the draft and the damper. Wind speed, mainly, dictated the settings of the controls, one of which, the draft, was a vane inside the chimney duct, while the damper was a hinged door in the side of the duct covering an opening to the cellar air.

If the wind outside was strong, the draft control vane

inside the duct was moved by a handle on a rod passing through the pipe and attached to the vane and the draft was set to a position partially blocking the flow of exhaust gases being sucked out of the furnace. The reduced rate of flow was reflected back to the air intake of the furnace, slowing it and thus reducing the rate of burning of the coals so that the furnace would not overheat. There was hazard involved in that too great a blockage of the air flow by the draft control would result in too little intake air for proper burning of the coal, resulting in dangerous emission of carbon monoxide, a lethal gas.

To avoid this condition, the draft control was set so that its interior vane would only moderately impede the air flow and the damper door was partially opened so that the pull of a strong wind outside would be divided between cellar air entering the damper orifice and the gases leaving the furnace pot. In this way, excessive air to the coals could be reduced without overly impeding the escape of the exhaust gases. (. . . I'm glad the days of the coal furnaces are past, too. I hope it stays that way.)

With the furnace tended to, I picked up the coal shovel, went to the coal pile, and filled up the bucket. The filled bucket was of such weight that I had to use both hands to pick it up by its hoop handle and to walk with it swinging awkwardly in front of me as my knees contacted it. Around the furnace I went, through the opening into the small cellar, and to the foot of the stairs. That's when the terror began, when I reached the staircase. At that moment the skin of my entire back seemed to be tearing off from my body as I became overwhelmed with foreboding, foreboding that something dragonlike was on the other side of the furnace and it was about to come around after me.

It was impossible for me to keep my back to the opening into the second cellar, and I turned to confront the terror. With the turning, the skin on my back came to rest, but my heart continued a wild beat and cold moisture oozed onto my brow. Staring wildly at the opening while I lifted the coal bucket onto the first step, then, with one foot on the first step and one on the second, I lifted the coal bucket to the second step, keeping my back to the staircase as much as possible. Then, being exhausted, I sat on the stair until I felt able to lift the bucket to the next two steps, standing sideward, as I went so that the opening to the second cellar was always in my sight. I could see part of the furnace through the opening.

After such ordeals, I felt disgusted with myself for being slave to unreasoning fear. Logic told me that the fear was groundless; pride told me to conquer it. So I did, but it took three more trips with the coal bucket. On my first try, I set the bucket down at the foot of the stairs; then I went back into the second cellar and walked to the far side of the furnace, saying to myself, "See; there's nothing here. There's nothing to fear." But when I returned to the staircase and my back began rippling, I had to turn around to face the nemesis. However, I went back to the far side of the furnace again in a second attempt, and returning, I tried to mount straight up the steps, but I could not.

On my next try, fear and I fought a terrible battle until I was partway up the staircase, when fear, having got a firm hold on both my shoulders, turned me around and sat me down on the steps. But on the third time down the cellar I won. I dragged my craven back behind me right up to, and through, the kitchen door. After that each ascent of the cellar stairs became less fearsome, though there always remained a slight residual of unease and a tendency to toss a backward glance, not of fear, but in defiance of it.

So, now for the finale of the campaign to overcome my fear of the dark. It was anticlimactic, as I have said, with no thrills of fear involved and only a mild apprehension. The next time I found myself alone in the house at night, I turned off all the lights and, once again, roamed all the rooms in total darkness, ending up in front of the cellar door. Without hesitation, I opened it and stepped through the blackness onto the small landing, then slowly down the invisible steps into the total darkness of the first cellar, through the opening into the big cellar, and around to the front of the furnace, which glowed a dull red. In a leisurely stroll, I moved to the coal pile, continued around the furnace to the second opening between the cellars, through it, and back to the staircase, where I sat down and calmly gazed at the darkness. Finally, I walked straight up the stairs and into the kitchen, where I signaled victory over unreasoning fear of the dark by turning on the light.

(... Is that all? What do you mean, "Is that all?" ...

We didn't have a walk-up attic. Access to the attic was by means of a ladder up to a trapdoor. But the attic was unfinished, so that walking about up there in the dark was out of the question. ...

Well, I don't know which would be scarier for entering, a dark cellar or a dark attic. Of course, you mean scary for you, not for me. ... You would be wary but not scary? Some night, when you're feeling bored, turn off all the lights in the house and decide whether to go first into the cellar or into the attic. I'd like to know your decision. ... I shouldn't hold my breath. Right.)

9

Homosexuality, Lightning, Ditties, Jokes, Tomato Paste, Home Brew, Anisette

Now, about ass. The big guys, in their discussions concerning women, would often inform one another that certain of their feminine acquaintances were: one way (specified), two ways (specified), or three ways, this last meaning that the lady in question would indulge in vaginal, anal, or oral intercourse, whichever was requested of her. Also, it seemed, certain of the women preferred their men in multiples, two or an indefinite more at a happening vulgarly referred to as a gang bang. (I would call it a sexual congress.) Some of such girls acquired nicknames such as Bang Bang or Boom Boom.

From time to time, the big guys spoke of homosexual men who chanced to be in the neighborhood. In such conversations there was an undertone of curiosity, but never of deprecation or intolerance. No judgments were made. In fact, on one occasion I witnessed a discussion held on the sidewalk among a group of big guys that included a homosexual who was in transit through the neighborhood and I was struck by the deference shown him. I inferred from such conversations that all the big guys had at one time or another indulged in the occasional invitation to homosexual intercourse, either out of curiosity or out of sympathy for the inviter. It seemed tacitly understood that all had engaged in some homosexual act. They did not ask each other direct questions about it, but I heard some of them volunteer the information that they had allowed themselves to be fellated.

Curiously, I noted, none stated openly that they had engaged in tandem in the anal act, which has a venerable history. Somewhere in the Bible there's a story about a very long military campaign that was spent by an army mostly in the field. When the army finally captured a town, they "treated the women as men." And the ancient Greeks were notoriously prone to this practice (and often prone for it). This Greek reputation for buggering, as the English call it, persists to the present day, as evidenced by a certain hostess's reputed set of party rules, one of which was: "No Greeks allowed in the leapfrog games." There is a maddening (to me) lack of clear-cut single-word description in the language regarding male-to-male anal copulation as to who is doing it to whom. Usually the male recipient of the penis is identified by saying, "He takes it in the ass," and the donor is described as "fucking [someone] in the ass." As for fellatio and cunnilingus, there is no commonly used single word for the donor of the penis or the donor of the vulva.

Well, enough of that for now. What else was going on while I was in the fourth grade, circa 1928? The talking motion pictures using the sound-on-film technique had arrived. Oh, yes, the lightning. (. . . Yes, I saw three forms of lightning then that I have never seen again. Let me describe them to you, OK? . . .)

Late one hot, sunny summer afternoon, I sauntered down the alley to the bocce court, where a game was in progress, intending to watch the men at their skillful play. However, something else claimed my attention, a strange and continuing lightning display off to the north, unlike any I had ever seen. At any one instant there were two, three, or more vertical streaks, which were apparently one inch wide, extending in parallel fashion seemingly right down to the ground. The streaks seemed twisted and of different colors along their lengths as they appeared and disappeared randomly. The effect was as though a box in the sky was being emptied of long brightly colored crepe paper streamers. It was a spectacular and beautiful sight with only brief intervals, no longer than fifteen seconds or so, when there were no streaks visible. The bocce players paid not the slightest attention to the display, to my wonderment, and finally I remarked on the lightning to them. They indicated that they had grown tired of watching it. At that point I chanced to look in the direction of the alley to the east and was stunned to see another, similar, lightning display at the distance of the horizon. A bocce player told me that it was heat lightning, as eerie phenomenon not only because of its appearance but also because no thunder accompanied it, a sparkling, silent spectacle. And both displays continued even after I wearied of watching them that bright, sunny afternoon.

On another occasion, I witnessed a quite different wonder in the sky, a single flash of lightning enduring scarcely a second, but what flash! It occurred during the aftermath of a rainstorm in late afternoon, while the sky was still overcast, so that the day was dark and the air was moisture-laden. I was standing on our back porch and looking toward the northeast sky when it happened. Over the big house located across the alley and at the intersection of the two nearest streets there suddenly appeared a huge, luminous chain—yes, a chain—of lightning. The perfectly shaped oval links each seemed to be about four inches long, and the whole chain appeared to be about seventy-five feet long and twisted in the rough shape of a script letter *L,* the bottom of which seemed scarcely five feet above the roof of the corner house. The chain was of a very bright, uniform blue-green color. One brief flare, and it was gone. I have no recollection of whether it had been accompanied by sound. But there is no forgetting that spectactular one-second sight so long ago.

And I witnessed one more lightning phenomenon, which, unlike the two one-time occurrences I just described, was on display so often over a series of years that I grew to resent the form. But once that type of meteorological show ended, I never saw anything like it again. The display consisted of two, sometimes three, parallel ribbons of orange-red lightning, each of which appeared to be about four inches wide, and they seemed to be about three feet apart. I assumed they extended from horizon to horizon, though I could see only the extent permitted me by the housetops. They resembled the long red-hot steel strips coming continuously off the rollers in a steel mill, except that they appeared immediately in their entire length and were extinguished in a matter of one or two seconds. But new parallel ribbons would appear, sometimes immediately and sometimes after long intervals, very closely in the same path and at the same apparently low altitude, and this went on for hours during storms. Occasionally, in memories, they still flash from horizon to horizon.

(I am too serious; how about lightening up a little? You know, I'm beginning to think there's more to you than meets the ear. You exhibit sporadic flashes of intellect that I find startling. All right, I'll lighten up. Here is some of the humor enjoyed by the kids, a few ditties and jokes.)

Recently I was strolling toward the corner of the block where the large sycamore tree grows when I heard a passing grade schooler singing, "Pease porridge hot. . . . " It amazed me that a song I learned in grade school was still not passé, and I mused on how many other songs might still be in the grade school repertoire, including out-of-school numbers such as:

No more pencils, no more books,
No more teachers' dirty looks.

(. . . You're familiar with that one. Did you know there are second and third lines? I just found out. They go:

When the teacher rings the bell,
Drop your books and run like hell.

(. . . You heard that, too. I'm glad that your grade school years weren't wasted.)

If, when school let out, the skies were sunny, the kids in the lower grades would often sing out:

"Oh, they don't wear pants
In the southern part of France."

After determined research, I discovered second and third lines:

Oh, they just wear grass
To cover up their ass.

There's the rendition of a present-day grade schooler (I vaguely remember having heard it):

There's a place in France
Where the naked ladies dance.
And the men don't care
'Cause they're wearing underwear.
There's a hole in the wall
Where the men can see it all.

But if on school letting out it was raining, the kids, on clearing the doors, would give vent at full throat to a ditty that must have caused the teachers to grind their teeth in rage:

"It's raining, it's snowing;
Teacher's ass is growing!"

The kids in the upper grades tended not to ditties but to word plays involved in comparisons that they called differences, apparently because they found it easier to say, "What's the difference between? . . . " than to say, "What's the similarity between? . . . " The questioner, after giving his auditor a brief time to guess the answer, would invariably answer his own question. It went like this:

What's the difference between a woman and a street?
They both have manholes.
What's the difference between a woman and an airplane?
They both have cockpits.

Later, beyond grade school, they said:

"What's the difference between a snake in the grass and a goose?
The snake is an asp in the grass. [Of course, a goose is a grasp in the ass.]"

My all-time favorite of this type is:

What's the difference between a group acrobatic act and a female chorus line?
The acrobatic act is a cunning array of stunts.

Also later on came the question and answer where definition in the superlative was involved such as:

Who's the greatest athlete in the world?
He's the man who can make a broad jump with his tongue.
Who's the most embarrassed man in the world?
He's the man who ate halfway through the hair mattress before he found out his wife was in the bathroom.

Eventually, the erstwhile grade schooler acquired the level of sophistication required to relate jokes involving a story. I'll combine two which were popular, but similar, into one story in my own words:

A rather strait-laced but nice matron had purchased a small talking parrot, which, it later turned out, possessed some salty vocabulary. As guests began arriving for tea one afternoon, the matron, who had forgotten about the parrot, hurried to bird's cage and, shaking a finger in its face, warned it to mind its language or be sorry.

The bird managed to hold its tongue until one of the guests accidentally knocked over her teacup, at which the parrot squawked, "Why, you clumsy butterfingers, I'll bet you can't touch your ass with both hands." In a fury, the hostess strode to the bird cage, removed the bird, and, holding it by its two feet, whirled it in circles above her head. The parrot spread its wings to the fullest and squawked, "Whee-e-e-e-e, feel the fucking breeze!" (End of joke one.)

The now-apoplectic hostess managed somehow to excuse herself, then rushed with the bird to the bathroom, where she wrung the parrot's neck and hurled it into the toilet bowl. Finally regaining her self-control, she returned to her guests and her tea party which turned out to be so enjoyable that by its end she had quite forgotten about the parrot. After the last guest departed, she hurried to the bathroom because she felt an urgent need to relieve herself, and she quickly sat herself down on the toilet bowl. The poor parrot, who was only half-afloat and in agony, had given itself up for dead, but at the shadow caused by the woman's sitting it still managed with a rapidly blinking one good eye to look up. It took a long look. "Wow!" it said. "If anybody can live with a gash like that, I still have a chance."

(I'm sorry, but I have to go back into the house again. I forgot to tell you about tomato paste. . . . For making macaroni sauce. I say macaroni [we rarely used the word pasta in our family], but we used the tomato paste to make sauce for all manner of dishes, including fish, snails, and meats.)

Imported Italian tomato paste was one of the few canned goods available at the grocery store and considered safe to eat, but it was relatively expensive, so we made our own when tomatoes came in season.

Bushels of tomatoes were brought home from the market to be washed and left to parboil on the stove. Meanwhile my father would take a piece of sheetmetal about eighteen inches wide and two feet long and, by means of a hammer and a heavy nail, perforate it at intervals of about one inch or less and then attach it to a wooden receptacle of the same dimensions and about three inches deep. The perforated sheet was mounted so that the jagged projections raised by the penetrating nail were pointed up on the outside of the box. The softened tomatoes were removed from the stove and rubbed across this remarkably efficient grater. The projections, which formed a rough circulet of sharp spikelets about an eighth of an inch high, served to remove the skin from the tomato and to allow the pulp and juice to strain through while impeding the seeds.

Then the strained-through pulp and juice was transferred to a cooking pot, spices were added, and it was cooked down to a moist paste, which could be cured by two methods. The paste could be spread evenly in a layer about an eighth of an inch thick on a broad, flat wooden surface and covered with a light netting to ward off flies. Every few hours, the paste would be turned by means of a spoon so that the curing would be uniform. The wood tray would be exposed to the sun every day for about one week.

But the other method of curing was less trouble. The paste was spread on a fine netting to which it adhered. A wooden framework, designed for holding washed window curtains spread out for drying, was erected in the backyard and the paste-bearing netting was attached to the dozens of closely spaced pins protruding from the framework. The netting was thus suspended almost vertically, so that not only was the paste exposed to the sun, but also to the air from front and back. Netting to protect from flies was added. A week of daily exposure sufficed for the cure, during which the paste turned black. Finally, the paste was spooned into a crock and spread into layers separated by layers of salt. It was ready to use for sauces, and it was there as needed.

(. . . Yes, my father made a very good home brew, tasty and robust. I'm not certain that gunpowder was not an ingredient; all I know is that his new beer exploded away a goodly portion of his bottles, often in the middle of the night, and usually with a report like a gunshot. I would estimate we lost 5 to 10 percent of the bottles. My father did not make wine, as so many of the neighbors did. But my mother made anisette. . . . Now that you mention it, that may have been illegal, but we never gave it a thought. We did not sell it; it was just for family consumption. But listen; I have good news for you. . . . It's the story of my first traumatic sexual experience—as a fifth-grader. . . . I tell you, I was traumatized. Just listen.)

10
Puppy Love, The Great Depression, Puberty

She was taller than I, and a year older, and she was in my class because she was repeating fifth grade. How can I explain being smitten with her? She was pleasant, personable, not unpretty, and not buxom; in fact, she was straight up and down. But in her presence I felt warm and weak, and in her absence I suffered without let a longing accompanied by a peculiar malaise. It was a generalized feeling of discomfort overlaying the front of my torso, as though it were a pillow against my body. It took five long months for this miserable disease to run its course, during which neither she nor anyone else had an inkling of my constant agony. Years later, I diagnosed my illness as a case of unrequited puppy love, a chronic, painful disease of several months' duration, with complete physical recovery, often with some gradually diminishing vague sense of loss.

This disease was to touch me twice more, but not as a victim. It struck in my eighth-grade mathematics class, just as the bell rang. As I rose from my seat, books in hand, I turned to my right to leave via the aisle, and I found myself staring into the eyes of the very pretty blond girl whose seat was in the next row and one seat back from mine. I felt two things simultaneously: a cold, sinking feeling in my abdomen and a stab of pity in my heart. For there was no mistaking that suffering look in those big, rounded, and widely open blue eyes. I recognized in her tortured stare that she was stricken with puppy love—for me.

But I had not the least feeling for her. I'm not speaking of affection; I mean feeling of any kind except pity. Strangely, I found her absolutely neutral, arousing in me no more amorous feeling than would a . . . a curbstone, a state of affairs that left me bewildered and distressed. As the days wore on, from time to time I would look at her and say to myself, *What the hell's the matter with me? She's good-looking, well shaped, and has a pleasing personality. Why can't I have some feeling for her, an iota? And she's crazy about me.*

But there was nothing I could do to alleviate her suffering. No matter how I tried willing myself to feel other than pity for her, it was to no avail, and the failure angered me. Once, I considered being merciful by simply touching her hand, but then I thought of the consequences of leading her to believe I was responsive to her affection when I could not be so. Sadly for both of us, the situation continued unchanged. I tried not to exist for her, and she pined for me till, at last, the school term ended and we met no more.

And here's a last tale of puppy love, in which I was not involved as a principal. This time it happened in Latin class in high school. Let's see; was it in first-year or second-year Latin class? Oh, it was in first-year Latin class. Know how I remembered? We were taking up the verb *facere, meaning "do,* make." And the conjugation for the singular of the present indicative active of the verb goes: *facio, facis, facit,* pronounced "fahk-it," which naturally puts one, everyone, in mind of "fuck it," leading to uncontrolled hilarity in the classroom.

In this case, the class grew tense with anticipation as the student called upon began to recite, "Facio," then tenser as he strained, "Facis," and finally, as he hoarsely blurted, "Facit," the pupils broke into a sustained tumult of those sounds produced when one tries desperately and only half-successfully to suppress his laughter. There were snuffles and snorts, gasping, choking, and strangulated sounds emitted through firmly clenched teeth exposed by tortured grins. Cheeks were brilliantly flushed, and eyes were bulging and watery. Though convulsed with this painful type of laughter, I directed my attention to the teacher to note her reaction to this disruption of her routine and found myself quite surprised. She had discarded her usual dour mien (sourpuss) and was standing by the side of her desk, relaxed, with a little smile on her face and a twinkle in her eye. Then it struck me that, of course, her view of the entire class in such a state must certainly be very entertaining. And besides, she experienced this at least once every year and so anticipated it.

Diverting my gaze from the teacher, I turned toward the source of strangled laughter emanating from the pupil in the seat on my right and was shocked to see a girl apparently in death throes. She was slumped in her seat with her cheek flat against the desk, her head turned toward me. One hand partially covered a twitching grin, her face was mottled red and purple, and her body and legs moved spasmodically. The sight almost caused me to stop laughing as I said to myself, *That poor girl's not going to make it; she's not going to survive this episode.*

But she made it; we all did after a few minutes of this muffled cachinnation punctuated by occasional twinges of pain. Finally, all that remained were a few random chuckles and silent belly ripplings. Four days later, however, this same girl was to suffer a different and more enduring seizure, less intense, but lasting for weeks. (. . . Yes, puppy love.)

I chanced to look idly in her direction during class that day and was startled at her aspect. She was sitting rigidly erect, and the eyes in her head were large and round, unblinking, staring, and luminous, like miniature automobile headlights. In following her stare, I determined that it was my close friend in the seat in front of me who, unawares, was being illuminated by those orbs. As an aside, he, even as I, had never paid any attention to this girl—let's call her Doris—who was, well, nondescript.

Anyway, after a few more days of her almost-constant staring at my friend's unresponsive right back-and-side aspect, I could brook no more. As the bell rang and we all rose to leave, I grasped my friend by the elbow and whispered into his ear, "Doris goes for you." (Let me hasten to explain that in the vernacular of the day this meant, "Doris goes into an excited state in your presence," with the connotation of simple fascination rather than sexual interest. To indicate her sexual interest in my friend, I would have said, perhaps, "Doris will lay for you." The word *lay* was also used as a noun, as in "she's a lay," "The Lay of the Last Mistrel," or "The Lay of Igor's Host[!]"

At any rate, when I whispered those words into my friend's ear, he turned his head and toward Doris and then turned his head away, both these actions occurring in the space of three-tenths of a second. I say three-tenths of a second because I read somewhere that the fastest human reaction time is about one-tenth of a second and my friend performed at the limit: one-tenth of a second to decide to turn his head in response to my tip-off, one-twentieth of a second to turn his head, one-tenth of a second to decide he'd seen enough of Doris, and one-twentieth of a second to untwist his head while expelling her from his consciousness.

The way things are between these two, I said to myself, *if by some chance they should find themselves alone in the classroom after school, and if she then should take off her pants, sit on her desk, and offer him her vulva, he would probably spit into it.* To spare myself the discomfort, I resolved to avoid looking at the unhappy girl. My friend needed no such resolution. For him, Doris did not exist.

(. . . So I made it out of grade school? Yes, you facetious bastard, I did. But before I did—in fact, just after I entered sixth grade—a cataclysm burst upon the world. . . . No, there was not a causal relation between my entering sixth grade and the catastrophe to follow. It was just one of those things that comes along from time to time in the course of history and upsets the whole scheme of life. Shall I go on? . . .)

The month I entered sixth grade, September of 1929, I read a banner headline on the front page of my local newspaper: "Stocks Higher Than Ever Before in History." Why that headline impressed me, an eleven-year-old boy, I can't imagine, but it did and I have always remembered it clearly. A few weeks afterward the stock markets crashed—and the succeeding ten years, with their economic devastation, would come to be known as the Great Depression.

Oddly, the difficult economic times did not snuff out laughter and enjoyments. Despite lack of work, scarcity of money, embarrassment and humiliation at having to accept welfare assistance, and concern for the future, there existed conviviality. Apparently, it was born of the almost-universal sharing in the social discomfiture. With unemployment rampant, there was a sense of nowhere important to go and nothing pressing to do that left people with time for each other, to gather and talk, to actually listen, to smile and relax.

For the young adults there was the big Saturday night with dancing to live bands at bars and clubs. For this they planned all week and dressed to the nines. Dancing started at ten in the evening. Often, traveling big bands staged outdoor performances on weekday nights, usually a Wednesday or Thursday, sometimes both. For the still younger, "shacks" that served as little clubhouses were constructed. In the field at a corner of the next block, earth was scooped out to a depth of two feet or so, and then a pitched roof of boards covered with tar paper was erected over the hole, which was large enough to accommodate five or six little kids sitting on wooden boxes.

At the cinder block factory two blocks away, cinder blocks were arranged to form a little room that was reached via a set of cinder block steps. Some shacks, built of boards and tar paper, were free-standing structures in backyards of houses. But the shack built abutting the back of my house was elaborate. My older brother and his friends spared no effort to make an excellent retreat, starting with a flat-roofed structure ten feet long, eight feet wide, and six feet high. The wooden floor was covered with carpeting. There was a stove for heating and cooking and table and chairs for dining or playing cards. Electricity was tapped in from the house to supply power for lamps and radio.

For my brother, his three friends, and me, it was virtually an extension of our homes for most of the depression era, a clubhouse par excellence. We even added an extension to accommodate a single bed, which I used often, lying awake for long hours while listening to the radio. There were broadcasts throughout the night by the big bands and solo jazz musicians, usually pianists.

Meanwhile, the economic conditions were rapidly worsening, and as more and more families were forced onto relief (welfare), including mine, some jobless were employed to work in areas that provided assistance to the needy. Unfortunately, such jobless were usually unskilled, while the work they were offered called for skill, such as making alterations on donated clothing or repairing donated shoes. A shirt altered for me had one wing of the collar longer than the other. Sleeves on some shirts were of unequal lengths. Sometimes the housewife in the recipient household could repair the damage, but often the clothing received had to be discarded.

In one egregious case, while I was in seventh grade, in junior high school, a pair of shoes provided me through welfare caused me considerable anguish. The fit was all right, but one shoe had a toe wider than the other. I could only surmise that two people had rebuilt these shoes, one working on the left shoe and one on the right shoe. I had no choice but to wear this pair of shoes to school for the time being. It so happened that, at that time, I was a monitor who stood at the top of the staircase that students ascended to the second floor, my duty being to enforce the rule against running up the stairs. What agonized me was that as the ascending students' heads rose to the level of my feet, their eyes became riveted on my disparate shoes. I tried not to squirm visibly. I'm not sure I succeeded.

And on top of that, along came puberty. Puberty is a form of puppy love for oneself. There's this constant urge to be doing something physical, but not walking, running, exercising, or playing games and certainly not working—chopping wood, for instance, or carrying coal. No, it's an urge to rub yourself against something, anything, until . . . until . . . you feel yourself getting warm all over, then quickly warmer, and then you're flaring! And with that flaring you experience an exquisite sensation of almost unbearable pleasure which quickly subsides, leaving you aware that you are expelling a bodily fluid, the emission finally subsiding to leave you first weak, then warm and relaxed.

But not for long. In several hours, the urge is there again, insistently demanding action. Well, in no time at all, the pubescent boy discovers how to gain relief without using a surface to rub against. Taking the matter firmly in hand, he goes to the root of his problem, his phallus, which he refers to as his cock or his prick, and manipulates it to the point where he not only feels his emission, but he can see it. He accomplishes this by grasping the turgid "tool" firmly and pulling up and down on its loose covering, or he slaps it from side to side, or he shakes it forward and back, or he covers it with his palm and rubs back and forth. This form of masturbation is vulgarly referred to as beating one's meat, jerking off, or jacking off. And the white blobs of semen that are emitted spasmodically and can fly a few feet at times are referred to, again vulgarly, as *jizm* (my spelling), or *come*.

Naturally, one does not keep such a sensational experience to one's self, so that before long, after discussion about it with one's pals similarly situated, one accompanies them to some private place where all can indulge in a mass jerkoff. My peers and I conducted this exercise in the cemetery two blocks away. We stood in an arc not quite a semicircle so that we could observe each other and yet have an opening toward which we could project our emissions.

Then the five or six of us began "pounding our meat" and observing our differences in time to orgasm, the number of emissions, and the distances achieved. There was wide variation on all counts, but there was an undisputed champion. He was not the first to "come," but his distance was amazing—I'd say six feet. And as he jerked and shook his sizable penis he would roar announcement of each emission, four or five in all, all the while grimacing and staring wildly. The only thing he did not do was froth at the mouth. I was impressed.

Not long after, in this cemetery, which the neighborhood kids used as a playground, I found myself without a companion with whom to play. An interesting tree caught my eye. It was high, and there was a long, almost bare, horizontal branch extending far out at a height of about ten feet. I worked my way to a point about halfway along the branch and lay prone on it. Suddenly that irresistible urge came upon me, giving me a hard-on (an erection), and I began "humping" (lifting and thrusting down with my pelvis) against the branch on which I lay.

Happening to turn my head to the left and looking to the ground, I saw the sharply delineated shadow of myself and the branch as cast by the late-afternoon sun. Watching myself in action as I humped added something to my relief efforts, something pleasurable, and I recalled this experience when next the urge came calling. So, at the next urging, in front of a large mirror wherein I could view myself down to the waist, I wedded my hand to my penis and watched my mirror image consummate the marriage. What should I call this form of autoeroticism? Self-voyeurism? Autovoyeurism? Masturbation se voyant?

(. . . No, no, it's not elegant just to say "jacking off in front of a mirror." True that's descriptive, but it's the custom to refer to such acts euphemistically and/or in a foreign language, as I have done. . . . There's nothing inherently wrong with the nontranslation. For example, which expression is the more intriguing, sixty-nine or *soixante-neuf?* . . . Of course, they mean the same thing. . . . You think sixty-nine says it all. You would. Well, let me change the subject.)

11

My Father, Church and Police, in the Hospital

One day my father kept saying, "That's two," and each time he said it he would cast a sidewise glance at me. I knew that he wanted me to ask him what he meant by that remark, but for some reason I felt irked and I determined not to give him satisfaction. He was sadistically patient, though, and all day he kept remarking, as though to himself, at intervals of two hours or so, "Well, that's two."

In the early evening I broke down. "All right," I said snappishly. "What's two?"

As though he had just said it for the first time, with no suggestion of triumph in his voice or expression, he quietly explained to me, "You have to get screwed three times a year." That's my translation of what he said in Italian. My father never—never—used profane or risqué language, no matter what his circumstance. He was a master of delicate expression. Everyone, he said, suffered three very aggravating negative experiences each year, such as injustice, frustration, betrayal, unfortunate accident, and the like. And, he said, he had just suffered his second such experience for this year.

Stupidly, I asked him what it was. I say stupidly because, even though interested, I desired a brief recitation and my father did not stoop to brief recitations. When describing something that he had experienced outside the house, he began his story with his leaving the house and continued with the path he trod and the events en route until he arrived at the scene of his screwing. He brooked no attempts to shorten his narration. Fortunately, he was a superb storyteller, and in this case I listened with both exasperation at his squandering of my time and fascination with his story. He never belabored a point. For example, there was no follow-up with a, "That's three."

However, he did try me on a similar tack, but I won that time, I'm sorry to say. What he did was to mutter, very occasionally, "Putanna de l'ostrica [whore of an oyster]," while covertly regarding me. Though very curious, I bit my tongue and did not ask him to explain. After a period of about three weeks, he ceased trying to get me to respond, nor did he ever mouth the expression again, nor did I ever ask him what it meant. Therefore, I have suffered exceedingly because I can't get the memory of the expression to go away and leave me alone.

To date, this is my best conjecture as to its meaning: In days of old, a vulva was sometimes referred to as an oyster, whether from its appearance or its taste or both. So, in those days, if a man happened to feel particularly venomous toward a woman, he might spit out, "She's a whore of an oyster!" Now if that's what the expression meant, then I have to take back my previous assertion that my father never used naughty language. But such language was totally out of character for him. There must be some other meaning for *putanna de l'ostrica,* and I shall seek out some old Italian men for assistance in finding out what it is. I have to know, or I'll never, never be happy.

(. . . What grade am I in now? M-m-m-m, I'd say

eighth grade, the year the blond girl fell for me in math class, 1932 . . . Sure, I can hurry it up a little. I'll have myself out of junior high school in no time. I mean—well, never mind.)

I had just passed the Roman Catholic church located on a business street a few blocks from my house when I saw them approaching me. In formation, in a column of threes, about thirty policemen in uniform were marching down the right side of the street, and as the head of the column came abreast of me, I noted that many of the marchers seemed ill at ease, embarrassed. I stopped to watch them. The column passed by me and arrived at the front of the church, where, to my great dismay, the marchers turned right and marched up the church steps and into the church. My dismay became rage. To me, this action implied that these public servants put loyalty to their private church above loyalty to their public office. After a few days had passed without any apparent public reaction, and I reflected on the statement the Catholic church had made by this action, I found myself thinking, *Where are the goddamn Protestants?* But there came never a peep from any source about the affair.

And it came to pass that it was my turn in the barrel so far as unnecessary operations go. (. . . You're not familiar with that expression? It's from a story about the sea: A novice seaman looked on interestedly as the sailors on his ship lined up on deck before an upright barrel from which the bung had been removed. The sailor at the barrel dropped his trousers, thrust his penis into the bunghole, and wiggled his hips about. Upon his withdrawal, the next sailor at the bunghole proceeded likewise. When the novice seaman asked what this was all about, he was told, "Just wait till it's your turn in the barrel." . . . Anytime. I don't suppose you need any help with the expression "he has me over a barrel"? . . . You do? I'll give you a hint. That's only the first part; the full expression is: "He has me over a barrel, with my pants down." Now do you understand? . . . You think so. Well, just to make sure you do, it means "he has an insuperable advantage over me," or as you would say it, "I'm gonna get screwed." Now, about my operation.)

I can't recall the symptoms that led to the removal of my tonsils and adenoids; perhaps I had the sniffles, or my toenail was ingrown. At any rate, I came out of the ether in the recovery room and was being restrained from leaving my bed, with the intent of getting a book to read. "I like to read," were my words to the attendants and relatives around the bed. But there was no book to be had. However, there was ice cream, the only food I could tolerate for the ensuing two days of nausea. Transfer to the second-floor ward followed.

There was at least one patient death every day in that ward during my stay of four days, and during one particular twenty-four-hour period there were five deaths. I'll excerpt a few episodes of that period, starting with a view of the room. The ward was high-ceilinged and rectangular in shape, the entrance being a doorway in the middle of one of the long sides. There were long windows in each of the shorter sides, and my bed was at the middle of the short side to one's right as the ward was entered. All the beds, fourteen of them, had their headboards against the walls, so that all the patients could see each other if the individual bed screens were not in use. As one stood in the entrance, bed number one was on his left, the numbers continuing clockwise to bed number fifteen next to the door, at the observer's right. The center of the ward was empty, so that the patients saw an expanse of polished wood floor.

(. . . Yes, I did say there were fourteen beds, but the thirteenth bed was numbered fourteen to accommodate the superstitious. I had to keep restraining myself from pointing out to the man in that bed that, regardless of his number, he was still in the thirteenth bed.)

I was in number eleven, next to an empty number ten, which became occupied about midmorning by a little elderly man. He lay awake and quiet, not showing any interest in his surroundings but gazing straight ahead as though in quiet contemplation. His bedsheet exhibited a high, rounded protrusion as though there were a bowling ball on his belly. After a while, he lit a tobacco pipe and puffed quietly while his hands rested on his chest. He seemed very contented. I ceased watching him and drifted off to sleep. When I awoke less than two hours later, bed number ten was empty.

I gazed thoughtfully at the empty bed, and as I did so, there came to my ears the wailing sound of an ambulance. Turning to the left, I looked out the window and down to the ramp that led to the emergency room. An ambulance had backed onto the ramp, an occupied stretcher was removed, and on it lay a young black man dressed very neatly with polished, pointed black shoes, smart trousers, and a white shirt that appeared starched and fresh. His hands were crossed over his belly, and his eyes were closed. On the left side and low down on his chest was a round jet black spot on his shirt, a spot about one half-inch in diameter.

Later, about four in the afternoon, a new patient was deposited in bed number one, next to the door. He presented an amazing apparition in that he was divided vertically into two colors, his right half being blackish purple and his left half bright red. The line of demarcation between the colors was distinct. He was an automobile accident victim whose chance of living was, I believed, slim. But he did survive. Interestingly, it turned out that he had been struck by a taxicab in which my brother was the sole passenger. As my brother related to me after my discharge from the hospital, it had been raining at the time of the accident when the man suddenly appeared in front of the taxicab. He was struck at full speed, and his body was hurled to the pavement with such force that it bounced up out of my brother's view, even though he leaned forward to see higher through the windshield. The victim came to rest about eighty feet down the street. Then, as I said, he ended up in bed number one, and survived.

But the saddest event of the twenty-four-hour period began that night after the lights of the ward had been extinguished for the sleep period and I had fallen asleep. I awoke to see that the area about bed number three was illuminated and that family members of the patient were grouped about the bed. Someone informed me that the man in bed number three had been subjected to exploratory surgery that had disclosed a hopeless cancerous condition. His wound was closed and he was given only a few hours to live. Because anesthetics were not effective for him, he lay in great agony while his family sobbed at his bedside in this open ward. At about two o'clock in the morning I fell asleep again while the man was still alive. When the first shift nurses turned on the lights of the ward at five o'clock, as usual, bed number three was empty. (. . . I'll be very happy to switch to a lighter topic. Note that I am now in high school, tenth grade, and it's 1933.)

12
The Times, Bordello Visits, CCC, First Job

The year 1933 was a tremendous one for the news media, as a profusion of significant events presented themselves. The new president of the United States, Roosevelt (FDR), initiated a string of novel economic reforms to combat the depression, Hitler came to power in Germany, and at the end of the year the United States ended its dry period of liquor prohibition with the ratification of the Twenty-first Amendment to the Constitution.

Fortunately, newspapers were very readable, making it possible for one to get the gist of many stories very quickly. This was possible because under the headline of each story there came first a dateline, which gave the date of the article and the identity of the news service reporting it; then, in bold print, came a paragraph or two summarizing the story; then followed the article in detail. Thus the reader had only to read the summary to get the main points and to decide whether or not to spend time on the detailed story. Would that this were the case today.

(You would like to hear more about sex? All right, I'll oblige, and then I'll graduate from high school, OK?)

One evening, I and some friends, all in our midteens, went to one building in a row of "cathouses" (you realize that *cat* here is a play on *pussy*, which, as you see in this usage, may signify the part or the hole—I'm sorry, the part, the female genitalia, or the whole, the bearer of the hole that is, the whole female. Shakespeare, incidentally, sometimes uses *puss* to address or refer to a girl or young woman.) Taking us in at a glance, the "clerk" saw that we were not laden with money and delivered himself of the ukase that only those boys who had money enough to "go," two dollars, could go upstairs. When he saw the disappointment of those excluded from the ascent into the bordello, he relented and altered his decree. Those not having the wherewithal to "go," he announced, could, upon payment in hand in the amount of fifty cents each, have leave to tread up the carpeted staircase on his right. So all of us climbed to the long and narrow anteroom on the second floor, where two of the boys "went" while the remainder of us sat on chairs along the wall to wait for them.

There were three slot machines along the wall, at the end of the room near the inner sanctum, from which emerged a girl clad in shorts. Her intent, I believe, was to induce us to deposit some of our loose change into the slot machines while we were waiting. She began playing one of the machines, and pretending to be angry at not winning, she began shaking and pounding the machine and calling it names, vulgar names, obscene names, sexually explicit names. I believe she had a secondary purpose, to arouse, by her words and actions, a possible holdout, one who had enough money, to the point where he would decide to "go." If this was indeed her ploy, it failed with me because, even though she did stand my hair up a little with her jiggling and pounding and shouting and she did widen my eyes at the complete abandon of her language, she overdid it when she gave the machine a vicious slap and called it a cuntlapper. It struck me as singularly inappropriate that a woman should so address an inanimate object, especially a slot machine. I lost the mood. Anyway, I didn't have the money.

(And now, as promised, I shall graduate from high school.... Thank you.... NO, I'm not having a party, but there is a table for gifts ... Yes, that table with the whiskey bottle on it. Pour yourself a toast in my honor. I said pour, not drink out of the bottle. You lout! I should graduate more often? Look; put down that bottle—on the table, I mean—and come over here and sit down. I'm going to postgraduate you.)

Oddly, the last half-year of high school was onerous for me. With no forewarning, a great tiredness overcame my being, and each school day I had to flog my recalcitrant spirit to push me against all desire to the classroom. Every day I was within a hairbreadth of quitting, but I didn't, and I graduated in the upper quarter of my class—into a world of unemployment.

Grown men in all categories of occupations had been without work for the last half-decade as I joined them in the (non)-workforce in mid-1936. Trudging from one to the other employment offices of the many industrial plants in the city in a fruitless quest for work led, after many months, to my enlisting in the Civilian Conservation Corps (CCC), a national reforestation program. The CCC provided jobs that afforded many youths their first opportunity to travel to a new environment, in any part of the country. I was not one of those easterners who ended up in a camp in Montana, or California or Texas, or Kentucky. My camp was fourteen miles from home, on the shore of Lake Ontario, and on a military reservation next to a U.S. Army infantry post, which gave our camp logistical support.

We enlistees were given a choice out of three work

groups: the pier gang, the road gang, or the tree gang, each under the overall direction of a civilian contractor. I chose the tree gang, whose director was a professional tree surgeon. We climbed and trimmed the forest trees of deadwood and felled and removed dead trees and stumps, and sometimes we removed live trees as part of a thinning process.

The road gang improved existing roads through the treed area and sometimes built stretches of new road. The pier gang constructed a series of long piers vertical to the shore of the lake in order to control soil erosion. These piers consisted of frames made of heavy timbers and filled in with large rocks and gravel.

Some enlistees were not assigned to a work gang. These were the mess personnel, the truck driver who operated off-camp trips, the mule skinner whose mule and wagon operated only in camp, the barber, the operator of the canteen, the firemen who in winter stoked the potbellied coal stoves in all the buildings, the supply clerk, and the latrine orderly. (The latrine building had three main areas, one each for washstands, toilets, and shower heads.)

There were two more people directly involved in this camp life: the company commander and the first sergeant. These two were army reservists called to active duty. The commander was a captain at the time of my arrival at camp, but he was later transferred and succeeded by a second lieutenant who was promoted to first lieutenant before I left. They had their offices in the headquarters building, where the three civilian contractors also had offices.

Behind the headquarters were the supply building and the latrine building, this latter having a space allotted therein for the barber. Then behind these two buildings was a row of long one-room wood-and-tarpaper sheds, the barracks, with a row of bunks along each side and two potbellied stoves spaced in the center aisle at one-third and two-thirds of the aisle length from the door. The bunk at the right of the door as one entered belonged to the barracks chief.

And the two remaining buildings were located at the ends of the row of barracks, the canteen with its store and dayroom (recreation room) at the left end as one left the barracks and the mess hall at the right end.

We wore army clothing. The members in a barracks comprised a platoon, and the barracks leader, who was ex officio the platoon leader, wore corporal's chevrons when in dress clothes. At work, the corporal was also the platoon's immediate work supervisor. For each set of three platoons there was an enlistee who wore sergeant's stripes. The sergeants assigned each platoon its work schedule and reported to the civilian contractors, who were seen only occasionally at the work sites. Both sergeants and corporals received incremental pay. Unrated members (we were not referred to as privates) received thirty dollars per month, of which we saw only six dollars, the other twenty-four dollars being remitted directly to our families.

On workdays, we awoke to the first sergeant's whistle, made up our bunks, made use of the latrine, and awaited the second whistle, at which we lined up in the open area fronting the barracks. There the first sergeant imparted information and instructions concerning matters other than work, usually. He always began by bellowing, "Men!," which I thought was very nice of him. At his dismissal of us, we made for the mess hall and, after eating, walked at will so as to arrive at our work areas by starting time. Except for lining up in the morning, there were no formations, generally. We did not march, nor did we drill.

My first night at camp was very romantic. After lights out, at ten o'clock, I lay wide awake in the very dark room filled with dozens of reposing enlistees like myself and listened to the whish of the wind, between the barracks and the creaking of the roof timbers. When I finally slept, it was a very restful sleep, a rare experience for me.

Of the acquaintances I made, the members from New York City were the most interesting, with their quaint accent and their almost-total ignorance of anything non-city. When one of them said to me during a trip into town, as we passed a herd of cows, "Look at the horses!" I believed he was joking. On observing him closely, I determined that he was sincere, so I corrected him and expressed astonishment that he could not tell a cow from a horse. He remarked that he had never seen either animal in New York City. But, I pursued earnestly, surely he had seen pictures of the animals in schoolbooks? He merely stared at me.

On another occasion, a New Yorker's bravado inspired me to enlighten him in an unusual way. There were four of us in the recreation room after lights out at ten o'clock, and we sat in front of the dying fire in the fireplace, conversing idly. A brief silence fell, after which talk turned to the supernatural. The New Yorker present stated that he wasn't afraid of ghosts, that there were no ghosts.

"Look," I said to him. "Do you want to see a ghost?"

"Yeah!" he sneered.

"OK," I said. "When you turn in, look in the corner of the barracks; you'll see a ghost."

"Yeah? OK, I'll look," he said.

When we met the following evening, I did not bring

up the matter but waited for him to mention it. He kept averting my gaze and half-turned away from me. So finally, I asked him, "Did you see your ghost?"

"No!" he said.

"What do you mean, 'no'? You didn't see a ghost?" I asked. "Did you look in the corner?"

"Yes," he said, shuffling his feet and with his head down. "'I looked in the corner for about twenty seconds—and then I stuck my head under the covers." Thus imagination does make cowards of us all. (Does that sound familiar to you? The remark I just made, does it ring a bell? No. Then you haven't read Shakespeare's *Hamlet?* You haven't read Shakespeare's anything. What a disappointment for Shakespeare, but he'll survive.)

For trimming a tree, three pieces of equipment were used: an ordinary, medium-sized handsaw to cut larger branches, a pole saw to cut small branches and twigs, and a long, half-inch-diameter rope. The pole saw consisted of a small curved saw attached at an angle to the end of a wood pole that was about an inch and a half in diameter and about seven feet long, an ordinary pruning tool.

However, the rope utilization was anything but ordinary. One end of the seventy-five-foot length was tied into a ingenious double-loop knot into which the free end of the rope could be inserted and pulled through or pulled back provided the knot was held in one hand and positioned to allow the slippage. If the knot was not so held, any pull on the rope caused the knot to assume a position that prevented the passed-through rope from slipping. The two loops did not slip, and they were used as a seat, one loop passing around the waist for back support and the other loop passing around the upper legs to be used as a seat. For comfort, we notched the ends of a board to sit on and forced it into the seat loop, holding it in place with nails bent over the notches.

We were allowed to choose our own tree from among those to be trimmed, and depending on the size and amount of deadwood, the task might take part of a day, the whole day, or occasionally two days. Unless there was a huge branch to be taken off at the trunk, only one trimmer operated per tree. A ground crew gathered and burned the brush removed and, at the call of the tree trimmer, tied to his rope end a hand saw, a pole saw, or a can of tar from him to pull up.

But first the tree trimmer had to get up there. There were four ways. The first step in each case was to enter the seat loops and to let the free end of the rope hang over one shoulder. Then, if the tree to be climbed had a very large girth and, which was seldom the case, a branch low enough to be reached by the seven-foot stepladder (normally used as a platform for sawing off large, low branches) the climber ascended the ladder and climbed onto that lowest branch. Usually he could then make his way up the tree.

But if that lowest branch was too high to be reached by means of the stepladder, say it was about fifteen feet high, the rope itself could be used to get to it. Starting with the loose end, the rope was folded back on itself to a length of about eighteen inches, then folded back to the same length three or four times more. Following this, the rope bundle was encircled several times with the adjoining rope so that now the bundle was shaped like a clothesline as gathered up for storage or as sold in stores, except that it had a long tail.

Now came the tricky part. Standing wide-legged and grasping the bundle in one hand in a manner to hold it together and with the other hand holding the rope in a loop with enough slack so that it just cleared the ground, the climber swung both hands back in unison to attain a long swing forward and up in unison, letting go with both hands at the top of the swing. If he was successful, the bundle went up and over the branch and broke open to a length perhaps five or six feet, which began to be pulled back by the longer length of rope on the throw side of the branch. The thrower quickly pulled the rope off the ground, lifting and snapping it to feed it over the branch with the help of the dangling free end. If the branch surface was smooth, he might fail; but usually there was sufficient friction to slow the rope's slide-back and sometimes even stop it.

Assuming that the climber was successful with the tricky part, he would then be faced with the hard part, climbing to the branch via the rope, pulling on the dangling free end to elevate himself. When I did this, something peculiar occurred. After a few pulls I would start to get an erection (penile), and if I continued, I would ejaculate. (That's exactly what I mean. Now that I think of it, I used to get somewhat excited when climbing trees in the cemetery where the gang used to play. Certain forms of physical activity do that to me, like housework, but I won't go into that just now.)

To avoid ejaculating, or simply to rest my arms, I would cease pulling myself up and would hold my position to rest briefly. (This was accomplished by holding the outside of one foot against the dangling rope, then hooking the rope with the other foot and drawing it under the instep and onto the top of the first foot, holding it in place by stepping on it. With the loop so formed being held in place by keeping one foot over the other, with the rope in between, the whole weight of the body could be allowed to rest on the loop without its slipping. All else that was needed was to hold one hand on the rope to maintain balance in keeping the body upright.

So, there I would stand, stationary in midair, until ready to resume pulling myself up; or, if I wasn't yet ready and the pressure on my instep became painful, I would reverse the foot positions and linger yet awhile. It was possible to pull myself up until my head was close to the bottom of the branch; then hanging onto the rope with both hands, I assayed to throw one leg up and over the branch if it was a large one, of it was not too large, I would throw both legs up and around it. Now the problem became getting to the top side of the branch. This necessitated, if it was a large branch, holding onto the rope with one hand while using the other arm and the legs to, somehow, wrestle around the branch to the top side. If there were twigs or shoots handy, this was relatively easy, but generally such was not the case. A clean part of the branch had been selected in the first place in order to have clearance for the thrown rope bundle to pass over it. If the branch had a smooth bark, the difficulty was compounded. Once I was on top of the lowest branch, the remainder of the climb could be negotiated with the little trouble, ordinarily.

(I feel my muscles aching; a little rest is in order here. Hand me the bottle, will you? Thanks. Now a glass—I don't drink as you do. And the water, if you please. Don't talk like that. I told you I'm exhausted. And there's some hard telling ahead. We're just coming to the medium-large tree trunks, so get rested.)

Now if the girth of the tree to be climbed was too large for the climber to get his arms around it but was of size enabling him to get at least his hands around to the side opposite him, a different technique could be used to climb to a sufficiently low branch, say about twelve feet above the ground. He embraced the tree trunk and while holding on drew up his legs and spread his knees, pressing them firmly against the trunk so that, by friction, he could hold his froglike position clear of the ground. With friction holding his lower legs in position, he could lift his body by thrusting upward with his upper legs, allowing him to secure a higher position with his hands and forearms, with which he again could draw his knees up to a higher clinging position. So that, like a giant tree toad, alternately thrusting with his upper legs and pulling with his hands and arms, he could move upward toward the lower branch.

Usually, he did not reach it. The great stress on the muscles suddenly employed in such an unusual way caused them to react with a swift paralysis. One moment the climber was proceeding with ease; then with no warning he was paralyzed to the point that he could barely hold his position, so weak that he dared not cry out lest the resultant slight motion of the chest against the tree trunk should dislodge him and cause him to slide down along the rough bark or to free-fall to the ground. When this happened, the climber's head would be at a height of about eight feet above the ground, and his plight would be quickly noted for the reason that this type of climb was not often used, so that it attracted spectators.

When the climber ceased moving and did not resume within a few seconds, a frantic search was begun for the stepladder and two, or more of the ground crew would position themselves beneath the stricken climber to ease his fall should he break loose before the ladder could be used to rescue him. Somehow, the seldom-used stepladder was always found in time, placed under the climber, and mounted by two people who supported the climber and put his feet into contact with the top step. With his legs straight, the climber quickly regained some strength, so that he and his helpers could slowly work their way down to the ground.

(Why didn't the climber use the ladder in the first place to get a head start? Well, as I said, it was used but seldom, usually as a platform for sawing off a large, low branch at the trunk. It would be stored some distance away in the ground crew's supply wagon. We just didn't think of using a ladder to climb a tree. The climber probably had not witnessed such an incident, or if he had, he felt he could succeed; or he may have successfully climbed some such tree to a branch at a lower height. Also, if he had his heart set on trimming that particular tree and his corporal would not brook the delay involved in locating the ladder and bringing it to the tree, he would have to climb it or select a different tree. Of course, he could have used the rope method to get to the lowest branch, but he probably didn't want to go through all that trouble if it could be avoided.)

Usually, though, the trunk of the tree to be trimmed could be encircled by the climber's arms and legs, making the ascent a matter of little difficulty. With his body in the seat loop and the waist loop and with the rope, as it came from the knot in front of him at his navel, slung over his shoulder, the tree trimmer climbed to the highest sturdy branch and pulled the rope up and over the notch formed between the branch and the trunk. Holding onto the free end of the rope as it cleared the notch, he introduced it into and through the knot and then continued to pull the rope through the knot till the loop over the notch became taut, the free end of the rope now dangling down to the ground.

Now he could stand on a branch, leaning back sufficiently to keep taut the loop between the notch of the tree and the rope knot in front of him, the support of the taut rope loop allowing him to maintain his balance while leaving both his hands free. He was ready to begin trimming the tree. At his request, shouted down to the ground crew, a handsaw and a pole saw would be tied to the dangling rope, which he would pull up to his position. After removing the saws and attaching them to his belt, he let the rope fall to the ground so that a tin can shallowly filled with tar and containing a small brush could be attached and be pulled up. The tar can had a wire hook by which it could be hung on the worker's belt or hung from a nearby twig until needed for tarring those fresh cuts measuring an inch or more in diameter. The tar prevented moisture from accumulating on the cut and perhaps causing the wound to rot.

For our purpose, trimming meant removing all deadwood from the tree. While the trimmer was close to the trunk of the tree or close in on a large branch, the handsaw was used to make the usually big cuts, and since stubs were not allowed to remain, two steps were necessary to take off any branch with a diameter of, say, three inches or more. Let me explain. If the initial cut was attempted with the saw cutting in line with the trunk (or large branch) profile, when the cut was about two-thirds completed the weight of the big branch would snap the uncut portion, but not cleanly, and by pulling down on it would strip the bark and part of the wood from that part of the tree trunk below it.

To prevent such injury to the tree, a big branch would be removed in the following manner. First, at a distance of about one foot from the trunk (or large branch) the dead branch would be cut upward from its bottom side and about one-third through, or to the point where the saw began to bind as the weight of the dead branch tended to close the cut. Then going to the top side of the branch, and four or more inches farther out from the trunk than the bottom cut, a cut was started downward, proceeding until the branch started to dip, usually to the accompaniment of snapping sounds. At that point, the trimmer began yelling, "Timber!" to warn the ground crew and others to stand clear of the tree. With added sawing, and sometimes without, and with a loud snap! the branch stripped itself away along a line from the bottom of the top cut to a point on the bottom cut and crashed to the ground, leaving a stub over a foot long on the trunk. To complete the branch removal, the stub would be removed with a profile cut and the wound would be painted with tar.

So much for the close-in type of work. Now it became necessary to go out along live branches, trimming and tarring as needed, to the point where the outermost deadwood could be reached with the pole saw. That point could be twenty or more feet away from the trunk on the nearly horizontal lower and larger branches.

To get out there, the tree trimmer stood on the branch and walked backward along it, while holding the rope knot with one hand in a position to allow the rope to slip through the knot slowly, his body pulling against the lengthening loop between the knot and the crotch high up in the tree. And when he arrived within pole saw length of the end of the branch, he would be standing on a narrow, springy portion that would dip and sway with each little motion of his arms as he extended the pole saw to reach and cut the dead twigs.

If there was a wind to further disturb his balance, he might have to interrupt his sawing from time to time to regain his balance and to avoid being tumbled off the swaying branch and, if branchlets didn't break his fall, hitting the ground or swinging against the tree trunk, depending on his distance out and his height above the ground. His difficulty was compounded when trimming after a rain or snowfall, because the wet bark could be slippery.

In fact, concern about working on one such cold, damp, and windy day led to a strike by the tree gang. The civilian contractor insisted that trimming be done even though the trees were wet and the wind came in heavy gusts. As the tree gang crowded together and began to walk in toward the camp, I found myself in the forefront, and looking back after a few minutes, I noticed that the group was changing from a compact cluster into a more extended configuration. In another few minutes, the group consisted of stragglers, some of whom were hanging back so far that they were still among the trees while we in the front were well in the clear and approaching the pier gang area. And when we reached the piers, there were only six of us out of the original group of thirty-five or so.

(No, unfortunately, I did not learn a lesson from the experience, if by lesson you mean giving up the struggle for a just cause.... I'm not starting to philosophize. You asked a leading question and I gave you a brief answer.) After the pier gang sergeant recovered from his amazement at our strike, he told us we could work with the pier gang for the remainder of the day. Actually, we were not assigned work—we would only have been in the way—and the work situation returned to normal the following day, no mention ever being made of the strike.

The year was 1937 and the news media were reporting on the severe drought in parts of the Great Plains, which were referred to as the Dust Bowl; besides that calamity, the economy was becoming more depressed. I had served five months of my six months' enlistment in the CCC. One day a professional tree surgeon came to the camp and offered employment for some tree trimmers. Two of us accepted and were discharged from the CCC to undertake this private employment. But special clothing was necessary for the job—breeches and shoes with knee-high uppers, which the welfare agency agreed to buy for me.

Well, I endured two days of private employment before quitting, not because of the tree-trimming work, but because of a conviction that I was in the role of a slave. I felt that my time and effort were being utilized not for some larger good, such as the preservation and beautification of trees, but for the good of a particular person to whose ends I was merely a convenient means, in a degrading situation. My newly issued Social Security card and I bid farewell, with no regrets, to my first civilian job.

Upon learning of my self-termination of employment, the welfare case worker, also known as the investigator, was understandably flabbergasted. She mumbled that this development could lead to the family's being denied welfare, but she would see what could be done. I took the matter out of her hands by joining the army.

(Yes, I'm starting on my way to Honolulu and the rendezvous I mentioned to you so long ago. Don't be so sarcastic. You would be amazed at how much I am omitting from this account. . . . I asked you to rein in your sarcasm. Now you made me lose my train of thought. . . . Wait; all right, I have it.)

13

In the Army, Invisible Blacks, Recruit Life

Since my CCC camp had been located on a military reservation and in proximity to the U.S. Army post there, I had seen soldiers count down, drill, and fire rifles and mortars and had been impressed with their neat uniforms and proud posture ("as though they had broomsticks shoved up their ass," the New Yorkers said), and I thought perhaps I should consider joining the army. Not long after, I was sworn into the army, assigned to the Air Corps, and on a swaying passenger train, taking me toward my recruit camp destination, which was on an island in Long Island Sound. There a series of profound psychological shocks awaited me.

I and about fifteen other new recruits were led down to a two-story grim brick building serving as a supply room where we were ordered to remove our civilian clothing and throw the garments into large disposal boxes. These civilian clothes we never saw again. An initial issue of military dress and work clothes included dress breeches and wrap leggings. The work clothes were blue denim fatigue outfits.

The recruits were told to don the dress uniforms. Then, after assignment to barracks and bunks, they received a brief orientation and were given the remainder of the day at their leisure, with permission to leave the camp if they desired. That was Saturday.

Early Sunday morning, at five o'clock, the recruits were startled out of their bunks by a barrage of shrilling whistles, which, I guessed, indicated some sort of emergency. I leaped from my bunk and ran to the nearest window, where I looked out into an early-fall day with a light mist in the air; leaves and twigs from a scattering of trees decorated the lush, green grass of the extensive lawn. Several noncommissioned officers were moving leisurely and at random on the lawn, seemingly out for a pleasant stroll, except that all of them had whistles in their mouths and were blowing on them loudly and continuously.

While I gazed in wonderment, recruit instructors—who were privates and privates first class—entered the barracks and ordered the recruits to don their fatigue clothes. These were blue denim outfits consisting of a loose blouse, loose-fitting trousers with balloon pant legs, and a sort of skullcap with a very wide, floppy brim. To me, it all smacked of the garb of a coolie. But even worse, the garments I wore were grossly too large. I looked and felt ridiculous. I burned with humiliation that I, a soldier, should be dressed thus.

Now the recruits were ordered outside, and my heart was further sickened. Almost unbelievingly, I heard the orders to pick up cigarette butts and any other trash around the barracks building. Soldiers at this menial work! The recruit instructors followed close behind while a circuit of the barracks was made by the trash pickers, who were then herded onto the great, damp lawn. There they were paired, each pair receiving a huge sack; to pick up leaves and twigs. Again the recruit instructors followed close behind, but this time, behind the instructors, were the noncommissioned officers, who would shrill their whistles to summon back the toilers to missed leaves or twigs. Early Sunday morning.

I found the kitchen police duty physically brutal and could barely stand on my feet after one of these fourteen-hour days: climbing up little stepladders to reach the rims of the huge five-foot-diameter stew pots where I would have to drape myself painfully over the rim to be able to reach down to clean the whole inside; upending uncounted wooden tables so they could be de-roached with scalding water and powder; righting the tables, then scrubbing the floors. On one occasion, an overseer cook, apparently fearing that I was about to drop in my tracks—which was a good estimate of the situation—actually ordered me to sit down for a few minutes.

By comparison with other fatigue duties, grass-cutting detail was a blissful respite. More than enough recruits were assigned the sickles to cut the grass near the outbuildings. Gradually the work crew would reach the areas on the far side of the buildings, and there the recruit instructors would become less impersonal, allowing themselves and the recruits to relax, rest, and converse. During such a lull, I overheard a recruit ask the instructor in charge of his detail about Negro recruits. He had not seen any, the recruit said. Were there any? The instructor appeared embarrassed by the question and lowered his voice when he answered so that I had to strain to hear. Yes, the instructor said, there were Negro recruits, but they were handled separately. The rest sounded garbled, but I gathered from a few words I caught and a pointing gesture by the instructor that the Negro recruit area was on the other side of the camp.

It took a little while for the shock to get to me. I was quietly reflecting that it was true, I had not seen a Negro recruit, when the instructor ordered sickles back into motion. As I hacked at the tall grass, my thoughts began a hacking of their own. The Negroes were kept apart, hidden from the whites. Their services to their country were acceptable, but they were considered unfit to mingle with white servicemen. I was disturbed. This was not democratic, not American. Then came the shock wave. But this *was* America! The United States Army—the United States Government was doing this. It was not the state of Mississippi, nor Alabama, nor Georgia, but the *federal* government! Incredulity then also swept me. The paeans to democracy that I had drunk in at high school penetrated my fervid mind, and I began to feel a sickness in my stomach, that sickness one feels on learning that his deepest trust has been betrayed.

Anger and sickness alternated in their attacks on my mind and body until finally my mind began an objective searching for the why of it, and the sharp sickness in my stomach softened into a feeling of emptiness. Finally I felt I had the answer: the federal government was kowtowing to the Congress, whose committees were dominated by Southerners. Congress held the military purse strings, and one price for granting the government's military budget requests was degradation of the Negro by the military service through the device of setting Negro apart from white.

For three days I agonized and pondered the shameful situation. What kept gnawing at my conscience was the same puzzlement and concern that had beset me in high school classes on American history and government when the teachers pointed out that all the most important congressional committees were headed by Southerners. This was so, said the teachers, because committee assignments were filled according to a system of seniority and

Southerners were reelected to office with greater regularity than Northerners. Thus Southerners became the more senior members. And they were more easily reelected, the teachers continued, because the South was sparsely populated, so that there was not the competition for election to office that existed in the North.

As I mentally scrutinized this disturbing scenario and subjected it to analysis, one aspect gradually projected itself as of paramount importance: the seniority system for determining committee assignments. And when I focused on that, all became explicted in the instant, a terrible, traumatic instant in which a series of tableaux, in logical sequence, raced through my consciousness.

First came the seniority system. Why would the Congress structure committees in a way that enabled members from the least populous, least economically developed, and poorest section of the United States to dominate its operations? The tail does not wag the dog—unless the dog wants it that way. That members from the poor, mostly rural, less populated, and politically weak South should exercise a dominant influence in the Congress over members from the vastly richer, more populous, and economically mighty North was preposterous—but it was so.

Now, why was it so? (. . . I agree. There can be no other explanation. But I wouldn't say it with those words. . . . Well, I would say that wealthy and powerful interests in the North purchased the services of the Congress. . . . No, not the whole Congress, only the significant and specially selected members necessary to exercise a controlling influence. Let me tell you how I reasoned it. The ingenious arrangement most likely operated in this fashion:)

A cabal of powerful northern interests (Your wry smile tells me that you find my manner of expression interesting—isn't that so?—please, unsmile; thank you) noted the stability of the official seats of many southern members of the Congress and decided to make use of it to exercise discreet control of the Congress. Using their more numerous northern member-employees as a control group, the seniority system was allowed to operate so that the senior southern member-employees could assume the committee chairmanships and other positions of power.

So long as they served satisfactorily for the cabal, they could keep their positions of prestige and power and were permitted to divert to their home districts and states vast outlays of public moneys in the form of construction projects and, especially, military bases. To serve satisfactorily, they needed to be the scapegoats for all sorts of discriminatory legislation and policies, and this meant that, though they were nominally Democrats to a man, they would have to vote with the Republicans on certain measures. And it was through their influence that low wages and racial and other discriminations were imposed and maintained on the country and on their constituents, for whom they were southern northerners. For the cabal, they were northern southerners, very handy cat's-paws. (. . . Yes, that's a very strange form of democracy.)

The next tableau, the next to last in the series, presented itself without delay, and with no less dismay than those preceding it. This tableau related to the press and its amazing inability to discern the undemocratic operation of the Congress and the racial discrimination by the government. Freedom of the press to address the public apparently meant freedom without obligation to print or not print and, when it printed, freedom to emphasize, slight, insinuate, distort, add to, or subtract from a story. Such freedom, unconstrained, would make the press more powerful than the government. Again, the tail does not wag the dog. The press restrains itself sufficiently to avoid open constraint by the government, and not printing is its major restraint—and its disservice to democracy.

And the last tableau, in the series that flashed through my mind upon learning that the federal government practiced racial discrimination, featured the public schools. How they spoke of democracy! Since they were governmental subunits of states rather than of the federal government, the schools in the North were able to be far less racially discriminatory than those in the South, where discrimination was integrated into the economic structure. Still, these northern public schools never explained to their students how a racially segregated South could exist in a "democratic" United States, nor did they ever mention that the federal government was segregated.

Of course there was discrimination and segregation and humiliation aplenty in the North, and not only for blacks. But the blacks were far and away the most abused in these respects. They could obtain only the most menial and most toilsome work. I recalled with poignancy the mass singing in assembly in Junior High School, "All the darkies are a-singin', massa's in the cold, cold ground." How must the very few black students have felt? Why did any students have to sing such a song of slavery in a "land of the free" and a "democracy"?

But I had to submerge all these thoughts and feelings. For the time being, experiencing basic military education was paramount. I enjoyed the daily stints at the huge drill field where the entire corps of recruits, except those on kitchen police or fatigue details, was together at the same time. They were in uniform, and the band played on their arrival, during mass drills, and on their departure. There were mass calisthenics with, usually, a corporal conducting the exercises. Not every day, but almost, the calisthenics instructor would apparently catch sight of an approaching officer, immediately cease the exercise, call the group to attention, and toss off a salute in the direction of our side and rear. I seldom saw one of these officers toward whom the calisthenics instructor would throw a salute, but I appreciated the subtlety and skill with which military courtesy was being emphasized.

The caliber of the entire group of recruit instructors was impressive. They were mostly privates and privates first class who had obviously been selected for their intelligence, alertness, and ability to work with people. Despite their hard driving, they managed in small ways to show human interest toward their wards; they were respected for their efficiency and fairness, and they were liked by their recruits.

(... Right, this is not the way recruit training camps are portrayed in the movies, but this is the way it was at this camp. Recruits were treated with courtesy. Voices were never raised to them individually; there was no verbal abuse individually. ... Yes, dissatisfaction with performance or work was always addressed to a group; no one was singled out for humiliation.)

With calisthenics completed, squads were formed and drill instructors held forth on the complicated, showy drill of the day. A "right about-face" took eleven steps to complete, with the pivot man rotating in place when the rest of the squad circled around him like a spoke on a wheel hub. "Echelon right" and other extended drill maneuvers called for the pivot man quickly to align his sight with two objects at a distance, one behind the other and, by keeping this alignment, to guide his squad forward in a straight line across the field. The inability of my squad's pivot man to make and hold this alignment subjected the squad members to some terrible physical ordeals, for dispersed throughout the drill field were sharp-eyed corporals who detected as many of these "awkward squads" as were necessary to unload the supply boats and empty the coal barges supplying the island camp.

The recruit instructors of the selected awkward squads were ordered to march their squads back to the barracks, where the recruits changed into fatigue clothes, and then they marched down to the supply boat or the coal barge. If it was the supply boat, the job was to walk up a small gangplank, take three or four steps down into the shallow hold, pick up a 100-pound sack or crate, carry it up the steps down the gangplank to a point about ten feet away, and repeat all this as necessary to unload the boat. The whole operation lasted—endured—an hour or two. For a squad of short men, and the tallest man in my squad stood about five feet, six inches (I myself stood five feet, four inches and weighed 126 pounds), it was a backbreaking task.

But unloading a coal barge was the nightmare job, long, unrelenting and grueling, for the barge was to be unloaded as rapidly as possible, since the army paid for the time during which the barge was tied to the dock. The unlucky recruits were issued shovels with which to transfer the loose coal to the unloading buckets attached to the moving endless belt. Ceaseless shoveling, interrupted only by marches to the mess hall for meals, was required of the recruits, who were continuously driven on and threatened by privates first class. One of the threats held over the heads of potential slackers was transferral to a small shed containing two unbelievably filthy toilet bowls. The recruits had been exposed to the shed and contents before they climbed into the coal barge and had been told that the toilet bowls were deliberately left soiled, to be cleaned by slackers as punishment.

Once, during a barge unloading, I felt exhausted to the limit after a few hours of continuous shoveling, and I rested my shovel on the coal bank, where I was maintaining an insecure footing, since the surface of the black mass shifted when disturbed by the shoveling. Immediately the nearest private first class pointed to me and stated that here was a slacker who was going to get into some real trouble, and where was the corporal in charge of the unloading?

However, the private first class took care to keep an eye on me while he raged and looked about for the corporal, and he stayed more than a shovel-length away, which was wise. For anger had banished my fatigue and I was seriously contemplating an attack on my tormentor with the shovel. Then I realized that it was not through coincidence that all the privates first class were huge, hulking men. They had been deliberately selected for their large size, I was convinced, to deter attacks by coal shovelers goaded to the limit. I resumed the work, which could hardly have been said to be interrupted, and no corporal arrived on the scene because, I reasoned later, that would only have added to the time necessary to unload the barge.

When the agonizing work was finally ended, twilight had long fled, leaving the moonless night to a few dim electric lightbulbs in the dock area. The bone-weary recruits crept out of the emptied coal barge expecting to fall in for the long march back to their barracks. Instead, they were assembled at attention in several files at the back of a nearby wooden building from whose wall a small lamp shed a dull orange light, emphasizing the darkness.

A corporal stood under the lamp, waiting for the last of the recruits out of the barge to join the formation. He was trimly uniformed, no blouse, wearing a campaign hat, and he was rather small. He could afford to be small because, being in charge of the entire detail, he did not have to get into the barge with the potentially hazardous coal shovelers.

As the last man fell in, the neat, trim corporal launched into a vicious tirade against the formation of coal-begrimed recruits. They were slackers, he said, lousy workers. They had taken fourteen hours to unload a barge, longer than any previous crew. The first sergeant would hear about this crew, he vowed, and so on, for about twenty minutes. I forced myself to submerge my feeling of hatred for the corporal, reflecting instead on how well he delivered what had to be a rote unloaded-barge harangue—and without notes.

I decided that, as a matter of survival—of my health, at least—something had to be done to avoid these work orgies. At the drill field, the next day, I made my move. While the squad was at a halt and standing at ease, the drill instructor was looking about to locate the corporals so that he might maneuver the squad away from them. As the drill instructor turned his back on the squad, I stepped out of rank and quickly walked over to confront the inept pivot man of the squad, looked him sternly in the eye, and said softly but fiercely, "Get out of there!" The startled man exchanged places with me and stepped into my place just as the drill instructor began turning to face the squad. To my admiration, he noted the switch almost instantly. However, he made no comment but resumed drill immediately with a simple march forward across the field—the fatal straight-line march! I picked a tree near the edge of the drill field and noted that it was almost in line with the corner of a distant building. I marched so as to keep that tree on the corner of that building, for a long, long time it seemed. The drill instructor was making a thorough test of the new pivot man. Apparently I passed the test, or perhaps there were no supply boats or coal barges to be emptied that day. But from then on, the squad was not detailed for any more unloadings.

(. . . Of course not. I had plenty of troubles left, but they were not so health-threatening as the hard-labor ones had been. They were more like exasperations. Just listen.)

One of the hard adjustments I had to make was to the fact that I was a small-statured person, one of the smallest in my new environment, and it took me a month to assess the situation in terms of people's physical sizes. On the drill field, there were plenty of squads composed of small men, but my bay of the barracks happened to be occupied by recruits who seemed to me veritable giants. Some originally average-height recruits grew taller almost visibly, gaining a pound of weight or more per day as they grew, rather burgeoned, before my astonished eyes. Their appetites were tremendous. I had known poverty, but these recruits ate as though they never had been able to confront a decent meal.

One of these big people was my friend who had enlisted with me, a husky, dark-complexioned fellow of Lithuanian extraction. His facial coloring fascinated me, not because it was dark gray, but because it was an absolutely uniform shade, so that somehow his appearance struck me as unreal, doll-like. He reminded me of a boy who had moved into my neighborhood at a time in my junior high school days, and his complexion was fascinating not only because of its uniform shade, but because the shade was white! He seemed to my eyes an animated sculpture of Carrara marble, a Michelangelo come to life but having the decency to clothe himself. How could anyone have such a complexion and be healthy? Yet he was very alert and active, apparently healthy as could be. I longed to speak with him about his complexion, but I never summoned up the courage, nor did any of my acquaintances. He was of English extraction. And he, too, looked unreal and doll-like. I would encounter yet another unreal, doll-like complexion many years later, in Japan, where some Japanese girls I saw had absolutely uniform cherry-blossom-pink complexions. To me they appeared devastatingly beautiful, causing me to palpitate and feel warm all over.

Of course there were some medium-size and small recruits in my bay, and I recall in particular the short, frail, wan-complexioned boy who told me that he had tachycardia. He invited me to listen to his heart. I put my ear to his chest and heard, not a heartbeat, but rather a heart flutter, at least three times as rapid as a normal heartbeat. The boy said he did not know why he had been accepted into the service in his condition, but now that it had been discovered he was going to be discharged because of it. It saddened me.

A few days later, a group in civilian clothes came straggling along the sidewalk as they followed a recruit instructor. They all entered the supply room, from which they later emerged in field uniform, and each held a book of coupons, an advance on their pay, worth two dollars in trade at the post exchange (PX), so that they could purchase personal items, especially razors and razor blades.

For they had been told that they would have to shave daily, even if they had never shaved and whether or not they thought they needed a shave. Further, they were now to get a GI haircut at the PX barbershop, and weekly thereafter. (*GI* were the identification initials for "Government Issue" items of quartermaster, as distinguished from items purchased locally at commercial establishments, but the initials were also used informally to mean "standard military" anything. *GI* meaning an enlisted man of the lower grades, as opposed to those of higher grades or officers, did not come into use until World War II. Up to then, we used the word *dogface* for this purpose. It was a form of whimsical self-abuse. Example: "A sergeant and two dogfaces are waiting at the gate.")

When I was designated to lead the new recruits to the post exchange, there was much craning of necks to locate me since I was lost in the throng, all of whom were taller than I. How could they follow someone they could not see? Thinking swiftly, I selected the tallest of the lot and asked his name. Then I said to him loudly, "You, follow me," and to all the others, "The rest of you, follow him." All of us admired my solution to the problem.

Came a day that I numbered one of the five happiest days in my life up till then. The Air Corps recruits were issued long pants! No more breeches, puttees, and wrap leggings for the Air Corps! I fairly danced with joy. Now, I felt, the dress uniform was dignified. (If only they would go further and get rid of those "coolie" fatigue clothes.) The recruits in the infantry, the Field Artillery Corps, the Signal Corps, and the Coast Artillery Corps were the objects of my sympathy in this regard.

14

By Ship from New York to San Francisco

Not long after donning trousers, it was time to embark on an army transport ship bound for the Territory of Hawaii. At this time, it was said that the army had more vessels than the navy, if the army counted all of its tugs, transports, utility ships, and minelayers. The troops were assembled at the pier, and when a name was called that soldier shouted out his army serial number and mounted the gangplank with his duffel bag. The band played, civilians stood about watching, and the transport wallowed lightly at its moorings. A few soldiers were seasick before the lines were cast off and the ship backed out of its berth. Soon the pilot boat put out a rowboat, which carried a pilot who would steer the transport until it was clear of the harbor. As they watched, the troops admired the courage of the men who ventured into the rough waters with their small vessels. The pilot boarded, and he maneuvered the transport out of the harbor in the wake of the pilot boat. And as soon as the pilot debarked to his rowboat, the transport was on its way and bound for the Panama Canal.

All troops were assigned canvas bunks below decks where the air was hot and humid and had the odor of rotting garbage. Some bunks were in two tiers with about three feet of space between them, and some were in three tiers with about two and one-half feet of space between tiers. One literally crawled into those bunks. The top man of a triple-tier had his nose less than one foot from the steel decking above. I, luckily, had a bottom bunk and lay facing the sagging canvas of the middle bunk.

Understandably, the troops spent as little time below as possible, leaving their duffel bags to occupy their bunks. They slept topside in their blue denim fatigue clothes, which were designated informal troop wear while in transit about the transport. I had spent a few hours below deck one night until about three o'clock in the morning, when I mounted the ladders to go on deck for fresh air. On stepping through the bulkhead door and onto the after well deck, I looked about in amazement, and my heart seemed to stop for a moment.

For all was either in silver light or dark shadow, both caused by the bright moon. And in the silver and dark areas were the sleeping forms of blue-denimed troops sprawled in various positions on the hatch cover, on the deck, on coils of rope, in the passageways. There was the soft rustling of the wind, the swaying of the ship, and all those still forms lying like so many corpses after a pirate raid. No one else was about; only I and the "dead," the moon, the moving ship, and the ocean. It was a marvelous spectacle, never to be forgotten.

But there were times, such as during the infrequent inspections, when the troops had to be below and by their bunks, and in field uniform. Such times were especially hard on those troops bunked directly above the engine room. There the heat, humidity, and odor were overpowering. On the decomposing floor covering was a layer of red slime an eighth of an inch deep, which condition made it very difficult to change clothes without soiling the trousers. Any piece of clothing accidentally dropped was hopelessly soiled. Fortunately, the inspections were very brief affairs.

As the transport droned on toward Panama at the speed of about eleven knots, averaging about 265 miles per day, the troops adjusted to their leisurely life at sea. The only duties required of them were to stand occasional inspections, participate in a few emergency lifeboat drills and perform one stint of kitchen police (KP) duty. But this KP was a positive delight to perform because the duty lasted only four hours and there were so may dogfaces assigned to it that there was no strain on any individual's part.

Each morning, at about six o'clock, some of the civilian crew of the transport would drag out large rubber-covered hoses and hose down the hatch covers, decks, and passageways. At eight o'clock, a bugler would precede the troop commander as the commander arrived to inspect the forward deck, the main well deck, and the aft deck. The bugler would blow a flourish calling the troops on the particular deck to attention, and the commander would pass through to the deck passageway leading to the next deck.

Not having been informed of this formality, I sat and stared on the first day the bugler blew attention while about me others rose to their feet. The bugler was a small, dark-haired man with beetle eyebrows that worked up and down as he silently made urgent speaking motions to me with his lips. The moving eyebrows drew my attention from the bugler's exaggerated lip movements so that I was slow in understanding his warning, *Get up! Get up!* I struggled to my feet and to attention just as the troop commander walked onto the main well deck. The commander took no notice of the late riser.

Usually, the remainder of the day was free. One could stroll, converse, play cards, loll about, read, smoke, or stare at the upper deck, which was the territory of the commissioned and higher-grade noncommissioned officers and their families. A canvas was attached to the railing, following complaints from the women, so that the women could sit discreetly at the railing and look down on the dogfaces below if they wished.

Often the sight of a woman at the upper deck railing inspired a soldier to attract her attention. I remember clearly the soldier who did a handstand. A handstand on a rolling deck constituted a feat that should have been applauded. It was ignored.

Though the voyage to Panama was smooth sailing under grayish skies, the civilian crewmen told the soldiers that it would be a different story when the Panama to San Francisco leg of the voyage would begin. The seas were always rough off the Pacific coast of Panama and Costa Rica, the crewmen said.

At last the transport hove into the Atlantic port of hot, humid Panama. The port metropolis, the troops were informed, was made up of two cities whose common border was the center line of the street. On one side of the street was the city of Cristobal, in the Canal Zone and under U.S. jurisdiction; on the other side of the street lay the city of Colón, in the Panamanian Republic. *Cristobal Colón* was Spanish for "Christopher Columbus," we learned.

After having been warned to beware of the Panamanian police, the troops were allowed ashore for the evening. There they, including myself, soon learned to tell Cristobal from Colón. The U.S. Military Police (MPs) were in Cristobal, and they would not permit any loitering by troops on sidewalks or street corners. If two soldiers stopped to discuss what to do next, a big MP suddenly appeared and ordered them to get moving. If the soldiers did not get into motion within two seconds or if they attempted to remonstrate, the MP took them into custody. It was best to seek refuge in one of the numerous bars, where the "reups" (reenlistees) and long-timers would give information and friendly advice to the new soldiers, and quaff cold beer the while. A "reup" was on his second enlistment, while a long-timer was serving his third or later enlistment. Both were called previous servicemen.

The foreign service enlistments, Panama Canal Zone (CZ), Territory of Hawaii (TH), and the Commonwealth of the Philippines (PI), were of two-year durations; domestic army enlistments were for three years. Most of the long-timers appeared to have had prior foreign service. Some had been to all three overseas assignments, and these informed the new men that the MPs in Panama were the "meanest" of all MPs. That was easy to believe, I thought. The Panamanian girls physically matured very early, the long-timers said, as did all girls in warm, humid climates. I had already been intrigued by some of these girl-women. I had also been somewhat shocked at seeing some of them obviously pregnant, for they just had to be in their early teens.

On the next morning, the transport began its trip through the Panama Canal, pulled slowly along between locks by means of lines to the little locomotives that were referred to as "iron donkeys." "We have to go south to go north after we leave the canal," the crewmen said. I had been surprised to learn that the country of Panama extended roughly east and west more than north and south, as I had always supposed. The course through the canal was southeast, but once out of the canal it would be necessary to pursue a course almost due south through the Gulf of Panama in order to round the peninsula of Azuero. Only then could the course be set northwest for San Francisco. And again the crewmen talked about the ever-rough waters waiting just around the Peninsula de Azuero.

But first it was necessary to pass through the canal. The average transit time through the fifty-mile-long canal was about eight hours, we were informed. Five miles from Cristobal, the transport arrived at a series of three locks that lifted the transport eighty-five feet above the Caribbean Sea level and onto the surface of Gatun Lake. Next came the crossing of the lake; thence proceeding up the Chagres River, past the small waterfall emptying into the canal and then along the dug canal through the huge Gaillard Cut, which was hewn through eight miles of Culebra Mountain on the Continental Divide. A great metal tablet in the side of the cut commemorates the feat. From there it was downhill through the Pedro Miguel and Miraflores locks to the twin cities of Balboa (Canal Zone) and Panama City (Panamian Republic) on the Bay of Panama.

When the transport left Panama's territorial waters, at the three-mile limit the ship's store opened up again and tax-free cigarettes could be purchased for five cents a pack. The ship's store was a godsend for the troops, especially for those who disliked the fare at the ship's mess. The store dispensed candy, popcorn, potato chips, canned snacks, ice cream, postcards, souvenirs, and toilet articles, including saltwater soap.

This last item did little to popularize the saltwater showers, the only type available while at sea. I took a shower, using the saltwater soap, but found I could work up very little lather. Only three minutes were allowed for an individual's shower; and one half-hour after the water was turned on, the water valve was turned off and locked. Few troops took more than one saltwater shower.

Languorously the transport moved through the peaceful, tropical waters of the Bay of Panama. Only when the ship began turning toward the north, around the Peninsula de Azuero, did a freshening breeze spring up. Soon the skies and the water began taking on a grayish tinge, and the sea became choppy and whitecapped. The ship tossed, shuddered to abrupt stops (it seemed), then plunged forward again, conjuring up the actions of a confused, frightened colt.

I happened to be working in the ship's library, that first day of rough water, when suddenly I became aware that everyone in the library, first-class passengers and troops, was staring at me with a sort of fascination. I was puzzled and somewhat annoyed at their actions because their attention was intruding on my sense of unusual well-being. In fact, I felt dreamily, deliciously marvelous. This wonderful feeling, and the staring at me by the other occupants of the library, continued for about ten minutes. And then it happened.

Smoothly, but quickly, the skin on my face drew taut, like a drumhead, I thought. Then, like a solid blow to the stomach, a feeling of nausea struck me, I *felt* green, and even as I dashed in furious haste to the short ladder, backed down it to the deck, and headed for the *leeward* rail I realized that what had attracted the open stares of the library patrons was sight of a green-complexioned soldier.

I made it to the leeward rail with the former contents of my stomach cramming my throat and fairly bursting my cheeks, so that I must have looked like a green glassblower in action or like a balloon inflator turned green instead of red with the effort. The impact of my chest's hitting the rail unleashed straining jaw muscles, and I hung limp while my insides exploded through my mouth into the leeward wind. The wind carried my white effluent stream out to a distance of ten feet from the rail as I stared interestedly through watering eyes. My nose was full of the emesis (vomiting).

But I was not long for the rail. Just as viciously as my insides had attacked from above they were now attacking from below. My abdomen seemed to be suffering deliberate dagger thrusts. Immediately after the next disgorgement, I fled from the rail and, reversing my field, dashed madly for the head (navy word for latrine) literally holding both hands over my ass.

When I reached the doorless entrance to the head, I hesitated to enter, desperate though my situation was. I faced the eight toilet bowls, which had no partitions between them, and gazed not at them but at some of their former contents that the tossing ship had caused to be ejected out of the bowls. The water on the floor (all right, deck) raced wildly to one end of the head to a depth of six inches and then back to the other end with the motions of the ship—a mad dash to the left, then back to the right, continually. The water was contained in the head by a barrier about four inches high at the entrance.

But my hesitation was brief. I staggered to a toilet bowl, with the water swirling around my ankles, and managed to seat myself just in time. My misery did not prevent me from considering that it was remarkable to make it "just in time" to the rail and to the toilet bowl. Something psychological was no doubt involved in such precise timing.

Then I groaned deeply as I entered yet another phase of my ordeal. My upper insides were preparing another eruption. I pivoted on my toilet bowl to face the bowl on my right. Timing to the split second, I reached out and grasped the adjacent bowl with both hands and pulled myself off my bowl to a point where my head was over the adjacent bowl. The moment I ceased regurgitating, I pushed myself back down onto my bowl—no easy thing to do when the ship's motion was tending to toss my body in some other direction. Soon I and the water on the deck went back and forth, in synchrony because it turned out to be easier that way.

There followed a brief, but damnable, period of the "dry heaves" (retching), or straining to vomit though there is nothing left to bring up. Perspiration was free, chills shook the body, and stomach acid burned the throat. That particular hell-phase over, I felt safe to leave the head, and studiously averting my gaze from the poor souls in the throes of what I had just experienced, I made for the open deck.

Once again breathing fresh air, I blinked my eyes dry and looked about. There were the choppy waters beyond the rail, and on the port side of the ship was the unusually short "chow" (any meal) line of troops for breakfast. Breakfast was served continuously until a half hour before supper, which was served continuously till the mess was closed for the day. Usually the long chow lines extended from the mess hall, which was forward of the main well deck, aft along the port passageways to the after deck and then folded back on itself. If one wished, after eating breakfast or the midday meal he could go immediately to the end of the line and arrive at the mess sufficiently later to have an appetite for the next meal. However, I was in no mood to take advantage of the relatively short chow line resulting from this first day of rough water, and I subsisted instead on snacks purchased at the ship's store.

Apropos of the word *chow,* I believe that U.S. Marines who had served in China brought it back with them and used it with the meaning of "something to eat." After U.S. troops entered Italy during World War II, Italians began using the word *ciao,* pronounced, "chow," as a form of greeting or, more often, in the sense of farewell. After pondering that development, I have deduced its probable genesis as follows. It is necessary to point out at the start that it is exceedingly hazardous to stand in the way of a GI (this expression replaced *dogface* when the United States began drafting civilians into the army) at chow time. So if an Italian wished to communicate with a GI at such an inopportune time, he would probably hear something like this as the GI rushed by like the wind: "I'm on my way to chow!" or, "It's chow time!" or simply "Ch- o-o-o-o-w!" This the windswept Italian would have taken to be a form of hurried greeting. On the other hand, if an Italian and a GI had been in the process of negotiating some quid pro quo when chow time arrived, at that instant the Italian would hear a loud scream, "Chow!" and find himself alone and staring at the rapidly retreating back of his co-conspirator. This exclamation the Italian would construe as an expression of farewell. After repeated experiences of these types *ciao,* as heard by the Italians, became adopted as part of the Italian language.

On the following day, I was to be treated to an amazing spectacle. The ocean off the coast of Costa Rica was as rough as it had been the day before off the coast of Panama. Not yet ready to join the chow line for the midday meal, I made my way to the after deck, which had a canvas cover over it at a height of about eight feet above the deck. There were two large coils of heavy rope on the deck, and a shipboard acquaintance and I settled ourselves onto them as though they were deck chairs, the large holes in the centers of the coils making it possible to settle in with moderate comfort.

As we looked out from the space between the canopy and the deck, the horizon seemed to divide the space equally between sky and ocean, when the ship was level for an instant. As the ship oscillated to port, the sky portion gradually decreased, then disappeared, leaving only water to be seen between the edge of the canopy and the deck. My companion said, "Look, no sky." As the ship began righting itself, sky became visible, increased to fill half the viewing space, and then, as the ship wallowed to starboard, it continued to increase till all was sky beyond the rail. At this point my companion would say, "Look, no water." He kept it up, "Look, no sky—look, no water—look, no sky—," until I began feeling queasy.

I suggested we join the chow line, and we did so, but with some difficulty, since the choppy waters buffeted the transport mercilessly and without let. It particularly distressed me when the bow buried itself into the water to the point where the ship's propellers came clear of the surface. Then the ship would vibrate noisily, trembling like a wet dog shaking itself free of water. Surely that was going to cause some seams to part. We could hear the crashes of breaking table chinaware as we came abreast of the open galley, which was separated from the port passageway by a wide-mesh metal screen. For some reason this same type of screen was installed at the rail covering the whole distance to the deck above and extending forward to beyond the mess hall (dining area). My guess was that the screen served to prevent galley and mess personnel from disposing of garbage over the rail.

Looking through the galley screen, I could see three

coal-fired cooking stoves in a line against the bulkhead, which was about six feet distant from the screen. On these stoves were cooked the meals for the first-class passengers (officers and noncommissioned officers and their families and others). One cook, a black man, had his back to the screen as he tended the stove on which was a large rectangular casserole dish, uncovered and filled to heaping with something, the sight of which caused the observer's mouth to water.

Suddenly the ship took a heavy list to port, hurling me backward onto the rail screen where I lay helpless, pinned by gravity to the mesh, which kept falling beneath me toward the churning water. The black cook was similarly spread helpless on the galley screen, and we both stared at the dishes and cups moving along the open shelves above the stoves, some of them falling out to smash in pieces on the stoves or on the deck. Then, very slowly, that wonderful casserole dish began to slide. I was located just behind the cook's right shoulder and was able to see his right eye go wide with apprehension; then his demeanor became one of desperate determination as he thrust to the casserole dish with the pointed poker he held in his right hand.

There was probably less than one chance in a thousand that he would succeed in keeping the dish from rotating around the point of the poker and sliding off the stove. But he held it! Unable to move his body, with his arm fully extended to catch the dish before it could gain speed, he held the casserole stationary on the tip of the poker until the ship came out of its roll, an elapsed time of perhaps five seconds. It was a miracle, and had I been Catholic I would have crossed myself. Being an atheist, I simply shook my head in disbelief, and I still do when I recall that magnificent riposte.

Finally we arrived at the door to the mess, where, looking in, I saw a huge cone of sliced beets standing four feet high at the far end of the serving counter. We picked up compartmented stainless-steel trays, had them filled at the counter, then moved to one of the dining tables. These were really long, high benches, parallel to each other and extending the width of the hall. They were two feet wide, covered with polished stainless steel, and about three feet high. As we were standing at these tables, our trays touched the trays of the diners opposite us at the table. By leaning forward a little, we could have rubbed noses with the opposing diners. My acquaintance told me that he had been sick at sea only once. That was when the diner opposite him at such a table had got sick and vomited into my acquaintance's tray.

Something peculiar took hold of me at the next meal. When I arrived at the door of the mess hall and saw that four-foot cone of sliced beets—it was there for the last two meals every day—I became nauseous. Upon my leaving the area, nausea disappeared and hunger returned, so it was back to the end of the line for chow. Again the arrival at the mess hall door, again the specter of the beets and nausea. There was no explaining it, especially since I liked beets. Unable to overcome this strange obstacle, I lived on snacks from the ship's store until the transport docked at San Francisco, fifteen days out of New York.

15
Fort McDowell and San Francisco

On landing, I counted two more physiological effects, besides nausea and seasickness, of a long sea voyage, one effect marked by its cessation and the other by its appearance. On board ship, there was the constant feeling of having a very mild headache, annoying at times, but usually barely above the threshold of awareness. This effect disappeared after one day ashore. But for the first three days ashore there were brief infrequent attacks of a sort of vertigo while walking. The ground remained terra firma, but I felt as though my body were swaying as though it were on the deck of a rolling ship. I would stop walking for the few moments it took for the sensation to pass. Apparently the semicircular canals in my inner ear (part of the organs of balance) had adjusted to the constant rolling motions of the voyage and were now readjusting to the lack of such motions.

This experience led me to ponder the vertigo sometimes suffered after heavy drinking of alcoholic beverages. How to explain that? Unless the imbiber were drinking aboard a rolling boat or ship, the only thing being tossed was the beverage, not the body. Why should the ear take offense? Yet I myself have lain with difficulty on a bed that seemed to buck like a bronco and held onto the sides of the bed to keep from falling off. It puts me in mind of a less successful drinker at Fort Slocum. (. . . Fort Slocum. The recruit camp—on Davids Island in Long Island Sound. . . . I didn't mention the name? Really? Well, now you know.)

The drinker in question managed to get on the ferry from New Rochelle to Fort Slocum and to make his way after lights out to the double bunk we occupied, me in the bottom bunk. He managed to undress and get up into his upper bunk, where he lay mumbling. Suddenly against the dim light from the windows, a dark shape descended from above and hit the floor beside my bed with a dull thud. As I turned to look at the inert form of my bunkmate, I felt sure that the five-foot fall was effectively one of eleven feet, if you count the six feet it takes to bury a person. All was still for one, two, three, four seconds. Then there was movement and mumbling, and the drunk arose from the floor, climbed up to his bunk, and stayed there, silently. What puzzles me in all this is that drinking off a stationary barstool can, and often does, produce all the symptoms induced by being on a constantly tossing platform: nausea, vomiting, headache, dizziness. In both cases, much remains to be explained.

After debarking from the army transport, we walked, carrying our blue denim duffel bags, along the Embarcadero, the street bordering the waterfront, to the ferry slip at the foot of Market Street. There we boarded the ferry that was to take us to a rock, named Angel Island, in the northern portion of San Francisco Bay. It was the site of Fort McDowell, a station for transients en route to or returning from overseas assignments. About halfway to Angel Island the ferry passed a smaller rock, on our port side, named Alcatraz Island, popularly called Devil's Island, the site of a federal penitentiary. On arrival at Fort McDowell, we picked up our duffel bags, departed from the ferry, and commenced a hard walk up the steep road to a gymnasium.

With relief, we set down our duffel bags and looked about the huge hall, which was dimly lit except for two areas, one at each end of the hall, and they were brightly illuminated with floor-stand lamps. The entire hall was filled with transient soldiers who moved freely about in the center after they had made their way through two lines, each leading to a bright-light area. We new arrivals were directed to join the nearest line, and as we slowly shuffled closer and closer to the lights, attracted as though we were moths, our curiosity grew as to what transpired there.

When I was five moths—I mean bodies—away from the lights, I craned my head to the right and saw a Medical Corps officer sitting in a folding chair. He was leaning forward. Two flood lamps, one on either side of and slightly behind him, were directed toward a point just in front of his face. When I was fourth away from him, I craned my neck to the left and saw a soldier standing almost at attention and facing the officer. At three away, by craning alternately left and right I saw that the soldier facing the medical officer had his trousers and drawers down and that the officer had in his right hand what looked like a snare drummer's drumstick.

At two away, I saw the officer striking about the pubic area of the soldier in front of him, in the manner of a conductor leading the orchestra through a presto passage. By beating about the hairy bush in this way—and incidentally setting into random motion the trio of the dangling genitalia below—he was able to detect the movement of disturbed crab lice, if present, in the bright light. In this case, some such movement occurred, and the medical officer yelled, "Crabs!" Whereupon two permanent party corporals (stationed at Fort McDowell) immediately seized the louse-ridden soldier's arms at the armpits and led him to the area in the hall reserved for delousing.

When I was one away, I watched with trepidation as the officer rather carelessly, I thought, slashed away as though he were clearing a jungle with a machete. I cringed at the downstrokes, which glanced off one testis or the other, and did not relish the idea of his playing fast and loose with *my* balls like that. And when he did manage to knock lightly against them I thought, *What does he think they are, chimes?* But, I supposed, after a few hundred such hurried examinations one can forgive the examiner an occasional slip of the stick.

At the other end of the hall, the pace was just as hectic. There the line formed to present urine samples for quick tests. I emphasize *quick* tests. There were two or three tests that were completed for each soldier within three seconds of his handing over his sample. In transferring the fluid from one vessel to another, time was of the essence, and urine was spilled onto floor, table, equipment, and tester himself with all the abandon of children engaging in a water fight. At last, the many hundreds of transients were processed in, and with their heavy duffel bags in their arms, on their shoulders, or on their backs, they were assigned quarters.

The five-day layover at Fort McDowell was interesting and pleasant. We had no duties to perform and were free to come and go as we pleased. At the small photography store I purchased some chilling photographs taken in China that showed beheaded bodies of losers in military situations, the executioners in military uniforms standing over them and wiping the blood from their swords. One picture showed a nude woman tied upright to a post with her feet clear off the ground. Her breasts had been cut off and a large piece cut away from the front of both thighs. Only the chin of her head, turned to one side, was shown. The proprietor of the store told me he had even more grisly pictures for sale, but I was revolted and did not seek to buy or even look at them.

I was reminded of a book that a classmate of mine in high school brought to school one day to shock his friends. The book's pages were of coarse paper, and it was a large and thick tome on every page of which were engravings of scenes of African tribal warfare, mostly beheadings. My classmate told me that his uncle had let him take the book to school, and since he was of English extraction, I surmised that his uncle had been in Queen Victoria's service in Africa and thus had an interest in such books.

Since transients from many different organizations were mingled in the small confines of the island, there was a profusion of different regimental insignia worn on their uniforms. These insignia were cloisonné enamel, pin or screw post, ranging from about an inch to an inch and a half in dimensions and usually in multicolor. If shirts were the uniform, the insignia were worn on each shoulder strap; if blouses were the uniform, the insignia were worn on each lapel. Some were beautiful works of art. There were some desultory trading of insignia, but one person became an avid collector and he inspired me to do so. In short order, with very little effort, I was in possession of eighty insignia before I lost interest. I made no effort to learn and record their identifications.

So that, when I eventually sought to organize my collection, it was dismaying to learn that there was no way to identify such insignia except through someone's personal knowledge, since there was no listing made of them. Apparently, each organization had been authorized to design its own insignia, which was manufactured by a government contractor who did not need to know the identity of the organization. And, apparently, there was no requirement for the organization to submit a report on its chosen design to higher authority, so that an unknown insignia could be identified, except for personal knowledge of it, only by looking into the historical files of many hundreds of organizations!

Of course, the main preoccupation of the transient soldiers was with San Francisco, especially with Market Street, which had the good sense to begin almost at the ferry's gangplank and offer all sorts of exotic drinking establishments. One of these I visited offered lesbian entertainment, and the singer rendered her own version of "I Used to Work in Chicago." (. . . You never heard of it? It goes like this [the first two lines and the last line are always the same]:

I used to work in Chicago, in a department store.
I used to work in Chicago, I did, but I don't anymore.
A lady came and asked for some drink.
I asked her what kind at the door.
"Liquor," she said; lick her I did.
I don't work there anymore.

    The lesbian singer's variant of this particular stanza went:

"Liquor," she said; well—you know me!
I don't work there anymore.

    And speaking of oral sex . . . (Say, you're more knowledgeable than I thought. I mean at times you seem less innocent than you undoubtedly are. But you're right—homosexual sex is not necessarily oral. I didn't say it was. Now, may I continue? Your knowledge of things earthy is sadly lacking, and I have been trying, as I go, to enlighten you to the point where you can function adequately when conversing in barrooms, barracks, whorehouses, smokers... You see? You don't know what a smoker is. Well, it is an old-fashioned term. It means a bachelor party, like his friends throw for a guy who's getting married. Now, please, just listen.)

Speaking of oral sex, the West Coast just teems with it. It's the sex of choice there to a much greater degree than anywhere else in the United States. I speak from hearsay, personal encounters, and readings on the subject (surveys, studies, reports). On my first visit to San Francisco, I was informed by someone (male) who chanced to be drinking at my end of the bar that oral sex was made popular on the West Coast by Scandinavian sailors, who had a marked preference for it. Their demand was quickly supplied by female specialists in sailors, such girls being adaptive, accommodating, and money-hungry. And the upwardly mobile girls among them popularized the practice at the higher social levels.

Because of the novelty of the city environment and the excitement it aroused in me, I did not waste time thinking about the alleged sexual preference of the Scandinavian seamen, though I was curious about it, and so the information was deposited at the back of my head, to be retrieved and mulled over at some convenient time. Eventually, after several mullings over a space of time measured in months, I theorized thus:

Long ago in Scandinavia, teenagers came to grips with the formidable problem of how to relieve themselves of sexual passions in the wintertime, when outdoor temperatures would often reach, say, thirty degrees below zero Fahrenheit. Since all family members with sense would be indoors in such conditions, a boy—call him Karl—and a girl, Brigit, say, could be alone with each other only outdoors, perhaps knee-deep in swirling snow. Penile–vaginal intercourse was out of the question, since they didn't dare expose even their noses for a brief time, let alone their asses.

As they stared glassy-eyed at each other, a sudden thrill of mutual understanding swept them. Though no words had been spoken, each knew that the other knew the common thought offered a solution to their problem. They could read the plan in each other's eyes as though it were printed there. He was to burrow down through four layers of pubic area coverings while she bent down with her head in readiness for the emergence of his phallus, which she would immediately engulf with her mouth, keeping it thus warm and safe until . . . until . . .

"I can't see myself doing that," Brigit told him tremulously.

"Just close your eyes," said Karl, "and I'll . . . "

"I mean that figuratively," she pouted as she knelt down in the deep snow and gave Karl a hand, literally, with his divestment.

So there you have it. Of course, Karl couldn't keep his mouth shut (nor Brigit hers), and it might as well have been the town crier who let the word out on sexual survival in Scandinavia in the solstice season. Gradually, the practice became eurythermal (independent of temperature variations), the teenagers became practicing adults, and many of the males became seafarers, some of them with ports of call on the American West Coast. Such sailors put their money where the girls' mouths were. Knowledge of this was spread orally, and the practice became so popular that with many West Coasters it's the only way.

En route to Angel Island, the ferry docked at Devil's Island (Alcatraz Island) for perhaps fifteen or twenty minutes to unload supplies for the federal penitentiary that occupied the whole of the island, affording me leisure time to scan the vista of the bay. Looking northward, I saw the turbulent water smashing against the steep and rocky shoreline, splashing up whitely to heights I estimated at twenty-five feet and more. At a guess, the currents were striking the cliff at perhaps thirty miles per hour. I imagined myself in that water, as a result of a boat accident, and trying to swim against the current as it rushed me toward the wall of rock. I shivered and put the thought from my mind, thinking instead how everything about San Francisco and the bay exhibited or implied motion and change: the swirling waters of the bay; the low, fast-moving clouds; fog hiding, then revealing, the Golden Gate Bridge as foghorns sounded on cue; the rise and fall of the slopes of the hills and the bustling streets on the hills, windy and wet. I summarized this environment, as I prepared to leave it, in one word—*dynamic*.

broom in his hand. He stomped down the aisle with his earsplitting whistle shrills interrupted by his shouts at those obviously awake and by his banging with the broom handle on the beds of those still motionless. When he reached the back doors, he turned and came back up the aisle in the same manner, except that now he overturned the bunk of anyone who was not at least sitting up. It was not easy for such unfortunates to tear loose from the covers that were held in place by the tucked-in mosquito bar, and the victim's thrashing about to break free from the covers that held him in suspension sideways to the floor, in his cage of netting, occasioned fury on the victim's part and difficultly contained laughter from the onlookers. In such manner were we awakened six days of every week. (We worked a half-day Saturday mornings.)

By work call, at seven-thirty, we would have shaved, showered, eaten breakfast, swept the bunk area, rolled up the mosquito bar and tied it to the support rod, rolled up the mattress to the head of the bed, and placed the folded bedsheets, the folded blanket, and the pillow on top of the rolled mattress. The bunks remained thus with the spring exposed until the end of the workday, so that if one wished to sit down in the barracks during the workday, say after breakfast and before work call, one sat on the spring (rather than on the low footlocker located on the floor at the foot of the bunk).

Sitting on the spring entailed a hazard because it sagged away from the bunk rail as a result and left an opening into which one's scrotum might dangle. This might happen even if one sat on the unrolled mattress while undressed. Upon one's attempting to rise, the relieved spring also rose, perhaps trapping the dangling scrotum between itself and the bunk rail, at which the unfortunate riser felt an excruciating pain as he came to the end of his tether, so to speak. There was no outcry because the pain caused the captive to catch his breath and to sit back down immediately, at which he would be instantly relieved and able to breathe again. Usually the pain lasted only as long as it took for him to stop bouncing from his fast sit on the spring and to gingerly retrieve his scrotum from the re-formed gap. I was caught more than once in this manner.

(Yes, I'm all right now; don't worry. And I was all right then. What do you think I was doing in that whorehouse where I met God?)

After the rude awakening and my ablutions . . . (. . . cleaning up—shit, shave, shower, and shampoo), I hit the chow line and arrived at that famous military meal, SOS (Shit On a Shingle), which is to say, chipped beef on toast. Then, following work call (poorly blown), I reported for work on the line. The "line" was the line formed by the aircraft that were parked wingtip to wingtip on the grass field as they were maintained or prepared for flight. I was assigned to a crew on one of the aircraft, which were Keystone bombers, Model B-4A. These were twin-engine, bi-wing, with an open cockpit in which pilot and copilot sat side by side. The wings and fuselage were covered with canvas painted a deep green-blue and protected with dope (shellac). They cruised at 110 miles per hour and landed at 60 miles per hour.

Working on the line was often dangerous because the spinning propellers produced an almost-invisible blur while the engines were being test run by the crew chief and his assistant. The remainder of the crew would continue their tasks, which might entail crawling under the lower wing, greasing the struts (braces between the upper and lower wings), or walking in front of the aircraft for various reasons—all of which brought one within a few feet of the transparent blur of the "props." After a short time of engine running, the engine noise was relegated by the hearer to a lower consciousness level, so that it was accepted as a steady background noise, only slightly bothersome. I thought it best to keep repeating to myself, *The props are spinning; the props are spinning* . . .

The situation was even more dangerous where the Martin B-10 and Martin B-12 bombers were involved. These aircraft had a narrow fuselage with two separate cockpits, one behind the other. They were entered and exited from the bottom, and it was necessary to walk between the two props to get to the hatch, let down a small ladder, and ascend it to gain the interior. When those props were spinning (and even when they were stationary) it was essential to walk straight forward between them on entrance to the aircraft and vital to remember to walk out straight forward on exit. For a big man, the tips of the blades of the spinning props were within a few inches of his shoulders.

Flying in the lumbering Keystone B-4A was enjoyable, especially since flight conditions were ideal: mild temperatures, sunny days with scattered cumulus clouds (seldom otherwise) and moderate winds. Since the canvas top of the fuselage was always kept rolled back, the crew members who were in the flight could stand at the sides and lean on the longerons (the structural metal tubing of the fuselage that extends along the length of the airplane) as though at the rail of a ship, and look down at the green fields of pineapple plantations as they slowly slid by under us. The viewing was excellent, as we flew at altitudes of about fifteen hundred to twenty-five hundred feet, seldom up to three thousand feet.

Sometimes the little pursuit planes, "peashooters" we called them, the Curtiss P-22s, and P-26s stationed at

Wheeler Field, would appear and swarm around us like bees, passing very closely above, below, and beside us. Some would climb a thousand feet above us and then dive straight down in a plunge that seemed to barely miss our wing tips. After a few minutes, they were off to other diversions or, more likely, went back to their assigned mission.

On some flights the copilot, wearing leather helmet and goggles, would twist round in his seat to face us. He would then raise a clenched fist and make pumping motions with his arm to indicate that he wished to transfer fuel from the auxiliary tank to the main tank. One of the flight crew would then grasp the four-foot-long wooden pump handle projecting up through the floor and work it back and forth until the copilot signaled "enough." Then we could resume our sightseeing. I enjoyed lying on my stomach and looking down through the open diamond-shaped hole in the middle of the floor, through which small bombs could be dropped by hand. I never saw mounted over the hole the bomb-handling mechanism for larger bombs. In fact, there was nothing in the body of the aircraft—call it the bomb bay—except a crew member or two and the fuel pump handle. I suppose the object was to decrease the total weight of the aircraft as a fuel-saving measure.

Meanwhile, on the other half of our island, the navy was operating with sleek flying boats, the Consolidated PBY-1s and PBY-2s, with which they daily patrolled for a distance up to two hundred miles out to sea. One more type of flying boat I might mention made a beautiful sight as it gracefully settled down on the blue water of the harbor and stirred up a long white wake behind it—the civilian Pan American clipper. It came in once a week as it flew its route from the mainland to Pearl Harbor, Wake,

Guam, and the Philippines and then came back from the Orient via the same stops. It was called the China Clipper.

(. . . Why should I hurry it up a little? You don't have anywhere to go, and you have much to learn. . . . Relax; sip your whiskey.)

Of course, besides working on the line, there were other duties to pull (perform), such as squadron duty, which could be Kitchen Police (KP), guard duty, and work details (trimming hedges, whitewashing rocks, sweeping streets, and the like). On Saturday mornings we would usually play soldier, donning uniforms and marching as a squadron with three platoons. For a few Saturdays the entire squadron was arranged by height, so that when viewed from the side as the squadron marched in column the heights of the marchers varied smoothly down from the tallest men at the front of the first platoon to the shortest men at the rear of the third platoon.

And as the third platoon, comprised of the shortest one-third of the squadron personnel, came abreast of nearby onlookers who were excused from the formation (cooks and guards), or were not squadron members (headquarters personnel and others), such onlookers tended to comment jeeringly about the short-statured platoon members. (I should dearly love to philosophize at this point. I've come to the conclusion that everybody in this world is some kind of a pain in the ass, and . . . Please, I know I promised not to, but just let me . . . All right for you. Just wait till you want something else from me sometime. . . . You're drinking my whiskey, aren't you? . . . I shouldn't have to bribe you to listen to me. I'm educating you, a very naive person, in down-to-earthiness, with emphasis on sex, ribaldry, and innuendo, in all of which you are seriously lacking, to the point of being nonfunctional in your milieu.)

(. . . How so? All right, I'll give you a little quiz. Do women fart? . . . You suppose so, meaning you have never heard a woman fart, correct? . . . OK, give me the context of this sentence, which occurs in a joke: "This time, leave out the part where the lighting strikes the shithouse." . . . It has to do with piano playing. Let's go on. What is the meaning of the expression "we're asshole buddies"? . . . No, it doesn't mean that at all. One last question: do you know how to play "lion" with a girl? . . . Congratulations, you have failed utterly. Poor boy, you have much innocence to overcome. How lucky that you have me to help you. Now, let's get back to the matter of the marching column and the taunting by onlookers of the third platoon, the last in the line of march and comprised of the shorter members of the squadron.)

The "Old Man" (the squadron commander), who was a young man, as were all the company- grade officers, and who was a pilot, as were all Air Corps officers (the nonpilot "ground" officers appeared during World War II), soon reorganized the platoons for marching as follows: one-third of the tallest men in the squadron were at the head of each platoon, and one-third of the shortest men in the squadron were at the rear of each platoon, and in between the heights of the men tapered smoothly from front to rear. Thus each platoon presented an identical appearance to an onlooker, and the overall pattern presented by the three platoons, as seen from the side, was one of serrations instead of a long unbroken line. And so the chance onlooker was left with no disparity at which to scoff.

Because of the mild climate, the uniform was "shirts" (that is, blouses were not prescribed for formations) and the organizational insignia was worn on each shoulder strap. Our insignia was a cutout of a winged death's head, the grinning skull in silver tone and the wings in gold. Under the skull and connecting the wing tips was the motto in Hawaiian: "Kiai O Kalewa," which I was told meant "Wings of Death." That seemed appropriate for a bombardment squadron, and it matched the features of the insignia, but after consulting my Hawaiian language dictionary, I made the motto out to mean "to watch from above." And this is very interesting because we also had a reconnaissance squadron in our group on Luke Field. So I believe that our group insignia was designed to reflect the fact that it had both bombardment and reconnaissance missions.

(. . . You're right, I apologize, and will speak more of people rather than events. So I'm stuck with people as a topic, since you won't let me discuss ideas [philosophize].)

The squadron area comprised a rectangular grassy quadrangle, as I have already mentioned, surrounded by one-story wooden structures. On one of the long sides, and paralleling a street, were the barracks and the orderly room, with their entrances facing each other, their entrance stairs being separated by only the space of the sidewalk between, so that each morning it took the first sergeant only three seconds to bound down the orderly room steps, cross the walk, bound up the barracks stairs, turn on the lights, and begin to shrill his whistle, shout, and bang on the bunk ends with a broomstick. I don't know how the orderly room clerk would be engaged during this matutinal rampage.

But the orderly room with its first sergeant and squadron clerk was really the anteroom of squadron headquarters, with its inner offices for the squadron commander and his adjutant. And one room of the building served as the squadron supply room. The supply clerk was a slim, blond private first class who was a sailing enthusiast. He owned a sailboat, to which he retreated at every opportunity, and one day he invited me to retreat with him for a sail on Pearl Harbor. That experience taught me that I disliked sailing on small boats as much as I disliked sailing on huge troop transport ships.

This latter activity was so undesirable to some soldiers that they reenlisted for another tour of duty ("re-upped") to avoid the ocean voyage back to the mainland. In fact, I mulled over doing just that myself. But I wished to see more of the world, so, I reflected, if I reenlisted, it would be for a two-year tour of duty in the Philippines, which was under U.S. control as the Commonwealth of the Philippines. But, on further reflection, I discarded that idea. I reasoned that since the Japanese were making great headway in their invasion of China, they would sooner or later overrun the Philippines. So when my "hitch" was up, I reupped for the West Coast instead, but I'll treat that later. (. . . What do you mean, you can't wait? Sit down. I'm starting to talk about people, as you wished. There's sex and God to come, so relax. That's it, but stop smacking your lips, will you?)

You recall I mentioned that the supply clerk was a private first class (PFC), one rank up from private. The army was so static then that a private rarely made (was promoted to) PFC during his first hitch; if he did, it had to be by kissing ass. On the average, it took eight to ten years to make corporal, about fifteen years to arrive at sergeant, and approximately twenty years to make staff sergeant. In the Air Corps, usually, one had to be a sergeant to be crew chief of a single-engine airplane and staff sergeant to be crew chief on a twin-engine plane. After the United States entered World War II, PFCs with one year of service became crew chiefs on B-17s, which were four-engine aircraft.

Well, I'll continue about the quadrangle, in a counterclockwise direction. On a short side there were the mess hall and the dayroom (recreation hall). On the Saturday following payday, which was normally the last day of the month, the dayroom was permitted to be used as a gambling hall open to anyone in the evening and up until three o'clock in the morning. It was mostly card playing for hefty stakes, and I heard that professional gamblers enlisted in the military service so that they could play in these month-end games, especially at Schofield Barracks, where the army population numbered about ten thousand.

Think of that. Honolulu was the only city of any size on the island of Oahu, which is about thirty-five miles in diameter, and all the army troops on the island received their pay on the same day. For two or three days, including payday, downtown Honolulu was shoulder-to-shoulder military personnel. Then, suddenly, and for the remainder of the month, the city was practically devoid of military personnel, their small spendable income having been squandered.

At this point, enter the "20 percent man," the soldier who loaned money to other soldiers. The loan, increased by 20 percent, was payable on the next coming payday and, if not paid at that time, resulted in the due amount's being increased by 20 percent and made payable on the succeeding payday. That is, the interest rate on a loan was 20 percent per month, compounded monthly. As in the case of the monthly gambling, this usurious money lending was winked at, both operations serving useful morale purposes for the money-short troops. I was told that some soldiers had enlisted for the primary purpose of engaging in this sort of money lending.

17

Loss of Virginity, Manual for the Courts-Martial

As a matter of interest, it was money borrowed from a 20 percent man that provided me with the means to go to town (Honolulu) about a week after payday and to deliver up my virginity, sort of. I had been conscious for several days that my testes were hanging low in my scrotum and were brushing against or gently nudging my inner thighs, to my discomfort. Seeking relief, I borrowed from a squadron member with whom I was in close association and who was a big-time 20 percent man (he had agents at Schofield Barracks) and I hied me to town, as they say in the fairy tales, and to (heavens!) A bordello.

Now, don't forget, this was more than a week after payday, so I had the whole city practically to myself insofar as the presence of military personnel was concerned. I ascended the inevitable staircase to the second floor and entered the empty waiting room, which around payday would be more crowded than a doctor's office. Immediately five girls charged out from adjoining rooms and stood in a row in front of me. Not a word was spoken as I looked over the pulchritude (Hawaii was a choice assignment for the girls, who were top quality and highly paid by the industry standard). I pointed at a very pretty petite blonde who instantly turned her back for me to follow while the four rejects immediately charged out of the room like fillies to pasture.

The room in which my rite of passage was to take place had a large window open to the street, and so it was bright with natural light. The little blonde removed two very skimpy pieces of clothing and lay spread-eagled on the high-mattressed bed, watching me as I disrobed. That done, I laid my body over hers (head to head, I might add) and, estimating that our pelvises were juxtaposed, I thrust downward with my hips. To my utter amazement, I encountered absolutely nothing that I could feel. I had apparently plunged into a vacuum. Four thoughts rushed through my head in quick succession.

First, I remembered a common saying in lowlife circles: "She had one so big, you couldn't touch the sides." *Oh, I thought to myself, then it can be true, and I thought it was hyperbole* (gross exaggeration).

Next I remembered another such common saying: "It was like sticking it [one's penis] out the window." What I had considered a ridiculous myth, I had now proved fact. It was exactly like sticking it out the window—that window, I said to myself as I turned my head toward the open room window.

Then I was reminded of the wisdom of the Indian chief—I can't say which tribe—who was reputed to have opined, with arms folded on his chest, "Ugh! Big woman, big cunt; little woman, all cunt." *Perhaps not always, Chief,* I thought, *but in this case I empathize with you.*

Finally, I was illuminated with a blinding realization that the void in which the universe was created was a void exactly like this one, an emptiness contained within a vast, primordial, loose vagina. Upon experiencing my experience, the Creator quickly overcame His dismay and He created heaven and earth within the cosmic vagina to pack it sufficiently for Him to feel that He was into a tight pussy. To arrive at a proper consistency of the packing material God found it necessary to keep altering and rearranging the Heaven and Earth components as He went, and it was six days before He got it right. He withdrew after one final and mighty thrust at the end of the sixth day, and He rested the whole of the seventh day.

Meanwhile, in the vagina, the end-product packing material, the stuff of the universe, most of which had been displaced radially from all points along the longitudinal axis of the vagina, continued to travel toward the walls of the vagina under three main influences; inertia, gravity, and vacuum. God had provided the initial impulse, inertia continued the outward displacement, and the mass of the vagina exerted a gravitational force that caused a constant outward acceleration of the shock wave in the packing material of the universe.

But God's withdrawal left a void in the vagina, resulting in a vacuum whose pull opposes the expansion of the universe and which pull, if great enough, could eventually stop the expansion, leaving the universe at rest somewhere in the intravaginal space. However, if the pull of the vacuum is sufficient not only to stop the expansion but to reverse it, the universe will at some time in the future begin constricting (imploding) and fall back to the longitudinal axis of the vagina, where the tremendous concentration of its matter will cause it to heat up to the point of explosion and reexpansion. This will lead to a series of constantly diminishing expansions and contractions until finally the matter of the universe will be distributed uniformly in the vagina.

At present, the cylindrical core of the universe, which had been occupied by the Creator's . . . —by the Creator—is empty and most of the packing material, as it continues to fly outward as a shock wave, occupies a relatively thin and dense cylindrical shell whose radius is expanding toward the vaginal wall as a limit. Let us examine the case where this limit is reached.

It seems that the universe is contained in a cylindrical shell, not a spherical or spheroidal one as the theoretical physicists say, whose diameter may continue to increase until the shell reaches the vaginal wall, there to remain attached, moving as an integral part of the vaginal wall. There will be no collapse of the universe, barring the use of some vaginal astringent. Only two questions remain to be resolved: What are the dimensions of this vagina? And whose is it?

With the passage of this last thought through my brain, I became aware of the very pleasant bodily warmth radiated by the person under me and upon whom I was now lying motionless. *Well, I thought, even though there is no packing to move against, I may as well go through the motions.* To my astonishment, I very quickly arrived at orgasm even though I was thrusting at apparently empty space. I had more surprise to come as I began to dress, for the young lady expressed considerable annoyance at my quick performance. Puzzled, I offered to repeat the act, but she haughtily rejected my offer, and even as she did so the reason for her annoyance occurred to me—well, one possible reason, at least. She was, I thought, suffering withdrawal symptoms after the sudden cutoff, after a few days, of the heavy action that began with the military payday. (. . . No, I suffered no trauma because of this case of the vacuum vagina. Unlike you I was knowledgeable about matters of this sort through reading and, while a kid, listening to the big guys talk.)

Before continuing this counterclockwise tour about

the squadron quadrangle, let me pause here on the short side of the quadrangle and mention what lay on the outside of the squadron area, beyond the mess hall and the dayroom. Looking outward and toward the right there was the hangar and the line (of aircraft), and beyond the hangar was the reconnaissance squadron, and beyond that was the swimming pool at the harbor shore. And beyond the swimming pool, in the harbor, there were always many naval vessels at anchor. I once saw as many as five cruisers tied side by side.

Looking outward and to the left lay the base library, with the harbor waters lapping almost at the door. Strangely, in my frequent visits, I never saw anyone else in the library, except the librarian. (At that time, in the year 1938, the average education level of army enlistees was that of a fourteen-year-old schoolboy, so I was told, which I supposed meant a ninth-grade level. However, the Air Corps required an enlistee to be a high school graduate. Another interesting statistic that I heard was that one-third of army enlistees were Southerners, probably reflecting the even more economically depressed conditions in the rural South than in the depression-ridden industrial North.)

And what was I doing with my library visits? I was reading the *Manual for the Courts-Martial,* which described court-martial procedures and offenses against military law. (. . . Out of curiosity. I had never read on legal subjects. And the reading could be interesting in that, amid all the dryness, there were the descriptions of sexual offenses and the associated penalties.) I tired of the subject matter and did not return to it until about a year later, when there was a new edition of the manual on the library shelf, and of course I turned to the sexual material, where a profound shock awaited me.

Additions had been made of minor sexual acts that were now listed as offenses, some acts had been reclassified so as to constitute more serious offenses, and the penalties had been increased generally. *What in hell?* I thought. *What band of bluenoses was responsible for these changes?* And immediately, I answered my own question: *Of course, religionists.* No other group, to my knowledge, was obsessed with sex as an evil and had the power to make military law reflect their view.

18
Dog Tags, God, Gas Masks

Well, perhaps the influence of religionists might be evidenced somewhere else to a certain extent. It seemed very likely to me that the Protestants were involved, in all probability in league with the Catholics, with regulations pertaining to military identification tags, commonly referred to as "dog tags." These were pendants on a cord worn about the neck of the soldier. (Naturally, a person wearing dog tags was, in a sense, a dog and the friendly insult directed at the wearer was "dogface," which came to designate, usually, an enlisted man in the lower ranks.)

This is how I came to the conclusion that Protestants and/or Catholics influenced, as religionists, a portion of the information carried on the dog tag: One morning, in the year 1939, there were gathered in front of the mess hall a small group of soldiers among whom was a corporal who seemed to be the focus of attention. Curious, I approached the group and noticed that the corporal was using a hand-embossing tool to punch information onto a metal tag. Upon my asking, I learned that dog tags were being issued to all personnel and were to be worn at all times, effective immediately.

What? Dog tags in a noncombat zone? In peacetime? Here, almost four thousand miles from Japan? Before I could unwrinkle my brow, the corporal looked at me. "What's your name?" he asked. I told him, and he punched it into the dog tag. "Rank? . . . Serial number? . . . Blood type? . . . Religion?" All without lifting his eyes from his work.

To answer his last question I said, "Atheist." He did not punch it in but remained motionless for several seconds with his head down, staring at the dog tag. Finally, he raised his head and stared at me, his eyes brimming with bewilderment. He remained silent and staring for several seconds. At last, he lowered his head, punched in that last item on the dog tag, made a duplicate, and handed both tags to me. When I examined them, they read: "Religion—none preferred." Not, "No religion," but "none preferred." I had to have a religion; I could not be an atheist. Though exasperated, I decided not to protest to the poor corporal, who was so shaken that he refused to punch out new dog tags when I pointed out that he had misspelled my first name.

And now I'd like to speak of God. (What the! . . . Don't bow your head, you dumb . . . Did you think I was going to pray? Are you out of your mind? . . . You were just checking the whiskey level in the bottle, were you? With your eyes closed, you were doing that? . . . You thought I was at the end of my preaching. I'd like to strangle you. All along I have refrained from moralizing and philosophizing. Do you consider my berating you for your appalling ignorance of vulgarity as preaching? My illustrative examples of coarse jokes, obscene language, lewd double entendre, etc., you consider as sermonizing rather than as educative? O thou of meager intellect . . . Never mind; let's get back to God.)

You will remember how I met God in a whorehouse as He was being hustled downstairs by two MPs and how astonished I was that He knew my name though we had never met. Well, it turned out that He had just transferred into my squadron a few days prior to that incident and had been assigned a bunk at the far end of the barracks. I met Him in the chow line the next day after our encounter on the stairs. (How did I know He was God? He told me.... Well, I took his word for it. I couldn't—and can't—prove that he wasn't god.... Of course I don't believe that gods exist, but I can't prove that. So if someone claims to be a god, I'll give him the benefit of the doubt. Ancient Egyptian, Greek, and Roman rulers and a modern Japanese emperor claimed to be gods. Who's to say they were not? The facts being unknown, one can only express belief or disbelief, or neither, about them. Unless facts indicate otherwise, I choose to accept, with reasonable reservations, that a person probably is who he says he is. The Jesus of the Bible was unlucky in that he did not meet many people with my attitude. But to resume about God in my outfit at Luke Field ...)

God wasted no time. He borrowed five bucks from me while we were standing there in the chow line, and it wasn't long before he was owing me fifteen dollars. My friend the 20 percent man confided that God owed him a considerable sum and had made not even a partial repayment in several months. I found myself paying for God's drinks in Honolulu bars in hopes that he would become conducive to answering some of my questions about certain passages in Bible, and I sought especially to have Him confirm or deny my theory on the creation of the universe. But God, like so many of the gods of literature, wished to talk only about drink and women. I borrowed heavily from the 20 percent man to get God drunk enough often enough for me to obtain sufficient material for a sketchy biography.

One day, in the barracks, God pulled His wallet out of His pocket and flipped it open to show me what appeared to be a policeman's badge pinned to the inside of one of the halves of his wallet. He told me that He had purchased it in a pawn shop and, by flashing it, had broken up a disturbance caused by two sailors in the crowded waiting room of a whorehouse. The grateful madam, convinced that He was a policeman and desiring to have Him handy for keeping the peace, gave Him a room in the brothel and also pay-free access to the prostitutes therein. He told me the name of the whorehouse, and when I visited there a week after His telling me this story I found that it was even as He had said.

Now, continuing my tour about the quadrangle . . . (. . . No, I'm not finished with God yet. We'll meet with Him shortly, on the fourth side of the quadrangle, in the latrine. . . . You don't have to go anywhere. Stop squirming, and listen.) There were some wooden storage buildings on the long side of the quadrangle, opposite the barracks and orderly room, and in front of these storage buildings there transpired an event that was vaguely vaticinal (prophetic). Three pyramidal tents were pitched there to hold the slow but steady influx of personnel assigned to the squadron.

It was time to knit my brows again. First, we were issued dog tags; now, squadron strength was being increased. And while I was still in the knitted-brow mode, another unsettling development ensued. A huge airbase was being built opposite Luke Field and along the entrance to Pearl harbor. I could see the dredges at work on the landfill for the future runways.

While this work progressed, I was moved into one of the pyramidal tents in the quadrangle, where my bunkmates turned out to be three congenial personalities, all of whom sprinkled their speech with unusual, sometimes startling, expressions. One of these that intrigued me was an expression for sexual intercourse, which use I had not encountered previously, nor have I encountered it since—*skizzle*. Certainly this is a cognate of *sizzle* in the sense of sexual warmth, as used, for example, in the phrase "a sizzling blonde," which now can be recognized as a euphemism for a skizzling blonde, and . . . (. . . You don't want to hear any more about words? . . . Just get around the goddamn quadrangle so you can leave? Well, all right, I'll hurry up a bit.)

The fourth side of the squadron quadrangle, the short side opposite the mess hall and dayroom, was occupied by the latrine, which abutted the barracks. To go to the latrine for a shower and shave, one left the barracks through the side entrance opening onto the quadrangle and, clad only in a towel wrapped around the waist, wearing clogs or sandals, and carrying a hand towel and toilet kit, walked left to the latrine, then right to the entrance at the center of the wooden structure. As he entered, he was faced with a row of washbasins extending left and right against a partition behind which lay the shower room.

To get to the shower room, one walked to the right, where he met a row of toilet bowls extending left, and walking along in front of the row, he came to the shower room entrance on his left. Between the entrance and the line of toilet bowls was a low bench on which one could leave his towels and toilet kit while he showered. There were eight shower heads, and the floor was concrete with a roughened surface.

One day, I made this trip to the shower room, removed the towel from my waist, and set it down on the bench with my toilet kit. Already on the bench were the towel and kit of someone in the shower room. He had just turned off his shower, and as I straightened up and faced the shower room I saw the sole occupant facing me. It was God, and He left me agape. His very dark skin gleamed, and He was sparkling all over with beads of water that decorated Him like an encrustation of diamonds.

Where I had thought Him rather frail, when clothed, His body now seemed solid, indeed powerful. And as I stared at His waist, my eyes widened somewhat, for He was well endowed. *He seems a satyr,* I thought, and as I did so I felt a tremor because even though my eyes were glued on His genitalia, I could see with peripheral vision that His tousled hair seemed to exhibit two tufts, one on each side of the forehead, like tiny horns. In a touch of horror, I thought, *He says He's God, but could He be the Great Deceiver?*

With a great effort, I forced myself to look down toward His feet. *If I see cloven hooves there,* I said to myself, *I'm not going into that shower room.* At that moment, I became aware that God had been studying me and had just moved His eyes to focus on my midsection. After a long look, He raised His eyes to mine and, speaking in a low voice with a hint of growl in it, said to me, "Hey, snowballs, throw me my towel."

Well, that remark infuriated me. I didn't go around remarking on the color of other people's skins, and I resented this remark on my skin color to the point that I lost control of myself. I hurled His towel at Him and snarled, "There you are, Eight Balls!"

Immediately I felt panic, for that's no way to talk to God (or the Devil, for that matter). However, nothing came of the exchange. I should mention here that God was not circumcised, so that I was spared the upset I feel when viewing a scalped penis. To me, a penis bereft of the covering of its glans presents an obscene spectacle. I shudder at the thought of parents permitting this senseless mutilation of their children, this foreskinning alive of babes at the hands of unscrupulous physicians who have now succeeded in making the practice fashionable for Gentiles.

This tirade reminds me that there were two of Jewish faith in our outfit, but I had never been in the shower room with either of them, and so I was not distracted from noting other genitalia of distinction. There were very few Jews in the service at that time, and these two were the only ones I had met, and since I had not seen their privates, as I have intimated, the shock of seeing my first circumcised penis lay in the future.

(. . . No, that's not it with God. There is one more episode. . . . You can't wait? You're leaving? Now? Near the end? Listen; hold on. I'll speed things up; I'll leave things out. . . . Come on; there's still a little whiskey left in the bottle. Hear me out. That's it; relax. There's a tingle of sex and God yet to come.)

About midyear 1939, the squadron received word that the concrete runways, the hangar, and the operations building and tower were completed and that we would begin commuting to work via ferry to the new airfield, Hickam Field. And, came the astounding announcement, we would wear gas masks en route and at work! This meant to me that Hickam Field was viewed as a potential combat zone! Once again I was overcome with dismay and disappointment at the government of the United States. *Apparently, the government wants war,* I thought sadly.

Soon the heretofore poverty-stricken squadron with obsolete equipment began to be lavished with new material. Some of the first all-metal bombers, the

Douglas B-18s, were shipped "knocked-down" (disassembled) to be reassembled on arrival at Hickam, and . . . (. . . No, wait. Don't leave. I'll depart Hawaii and go back to the mainland, OK? I was at that point anyway, because I left the territory at the end of 1939. OK?)

19
In California, Japanese Attack Hawaii, March Field, Debtor God

As I told you, reenlisting for a hitch in the Philippines was too risky, in my opinion, because of the Japanese military expansion in the Orient. So I reupped on the West Coast and was assigned to a transport squadron at the Sacramento Air Depot. We flew supplies to and from Air Corps facilities in the West with our Douglas DC-3 aircraft. And that's where I was when the Japanese bombed Pearl Harbor, the seventh of December 1941.

For ten days following the attack on Pearl Harbor we operated at the depot on an around-the-clock work schedule; then suddenly we reverted to our normal pre–Pearl Harbor work schedules as though the attack had not occurred. No new equipment or supplies of any kind were in evidence. Everything was perfectly peacetime normal.

But everything was perfectly abnormal at March Field, west of Los Angeles at Riverside, California, as I discovered a short time later. I was detailed there as radio operator and mechanic on an empty DC-3 with a crew of three—the pilot, the copilot, and me.

As we flew into the huge bomber base, I was stunned to discover that there were no aircraft there! March Field was deserted except for caretaker personnel. We parked our sole aircraft in the center of this vast emptiness, on the runway and in position for takeoff. A motor vehicle was dispatched to carry us into the hangar area, and as we rode in, a pursuit plane landed and taxied in to the hangar apron. Now there were two aircraft on March Field, an empty transport and a pursuit plane.

My routine for the next several days of my assignment was only to "pull" a radio check each morning on the empty transport standing always ready for takeoff. To do this task, I had to check out as a driver of a two-and-one-half ton truck, apparently the only vehicle available for me, to drive out to the DC-3. There were at least two pursuit planes operating that I saw at any one time, perhaps three, because their object seemed to be to have one of them in the air at all times. Obviously, they were acting as lookouts and, obviously, the DC-3 was standing by to evacuate certain personnel, I didn't know who, when the lookout sounded the alert.

(Don't look at me like that. Of course I'm going to tell you what I surmised from all that, and I think you will be surprised and consternated by it. Well, maybe surprised, anyway.)

As I pondered all this (you knew I was going to ponder all this), it became quite clear to me that the United States had abandoned the defense of the West Coast. If March Field, the biggest, was evacuated, surely no other airfields on the Coast would be combat-operational. If the Japanese wished to attack, they had carte blanche. *Well,* I thought, *what about the Panama Canal?* Was Albrook Field, in Panama, already evacuated? Of course. It had to be. If the United States couldn't defend the West Coast, it couldn't defend the canal.

When we returned to the Sacramento Air Depot after about a week, we made no mention of the state of affairs at March Field. We had not been advised not to comment on it, and I don't know why we didn't—at least I didn't comment on it. Nor was there a word on radio or in newspaper on it. But as I looked about me, at the personnel of the depot and, when in town, at the people of Sacramento, I wondered what they would think if they knew, as I thought I knew, that they had been abandoned to possible bombing by the enemy.

Now, about God again. Not long ago, in New York City, I happened to meet the 20 percent man who had been in my squadron in Hawaii so long ago. And I jokingly asked him whether he had ever collected on his loans to God. His face darkened and his eyes became steely. "That Deadbeat, . . . " he began, then checked himself. "I haven't thought about Him in a long time. You know, shortly after you left the islands, God went over the hill [deserted]. He stowed away on one of the two luxury liners that sailed between the coast and the islands, and the last I heard about Him was that He was working as a waiter-entertainer in a transvestite joint on Market Street in San Francisco. He wore a long dress, bare at the shoulders and low-cut in the back. At intervals, He would stop waiting on tables, ascend the steps to the stage, and sing solo numbers.

"But now that you mention it, let's see how much He owes me," and the 20 percent man pulled a hand-sized electronic business calculator out of his pocket "Let's see, now. Two hundred and seventy dollars—how did I let Him get into me for that much?—at twenty percent compounded monthly for . . . for fifty years is . . . Why, that son of a bitch! He owes me $5,477,721.85! I'll kill Him! I'm offering a reward—twenty percent; that's over a million dollars—to anyone who leads me to God, providing I collect, of course."

(Wait a minute. Where are you going? You can't leave

now. . . . But you're too innocent to function. You haven't learned enough about sex, swearing, suggestion. . . . You don't know about "don't make waves!" You don't know about, "Where were you when the shit hit the fan?" Stop! You're too callow. Come back, you hear? Come back!)